CHI-TOWN

DREGS OF SOCIETY

WILLIAM E. WILSON

ARCHWAY
PUBLISHING

Archway Publishing books may be ordered through booksellers or by contacting:

Archway Publishing
1663 Liberty Drive
Bloomington, IN 47403
www.archwaypublishing.com
844-669-3957

ISBN: 978-1-4808-9873-8 (sc)
ISBN: 978-1-4808-9872-1 (hc)
ISBN: 978-1-4808-9874-5 (e)

Library of Congress Control Number: 2020921458

Print information available on the last page.

Archway Publishing rev. date: 11/20/2020

CONTENTS

PROLOGUE

Chicago was incorporated in 1837. Later, the fledging town literally was mud jacked from the swamplands it sat on and eventually implemented its own police presence sometime in the 1850s. The boomtown with its ragtag group of law enforcement officers took on a life of its own and still struggles with many of the same issues today.

From its humble beginnings, Chicago has been home to some of the most famous and notable crime figures in American history. Law enforcement agencies in Chicago still face the same problems. With continuous corruption by certain local elected politicians and exploitation of a small number of police, lawlessness, disorder, and mayhem continue running wild and uncontainable. Will Chicagoans ever learn?

In the late 1800s and early 1900s, notable underworld figures came crawling out of the woodwork, appeared in the Windy City, and brought with them corruption and exploitation. Roger Plant, an immigrant from England, established the first house of ill repute, the Under the Willows whorehouse. From this modest beginning, this criminal practice got its start and quickly made its presence known in Mud City or Chi-Town as it is now frequently referred to.

Michael "Hinky Dink" Kenna and "Bathhouse John" Coughlin were an unlikely pair who appeared on the scene around that time. They were total opposites; Hinky Dink was very low key and passive while Bathhouse John was flamboyant and lively. They were two of the most memorable and colorful men born around the 1850s and later become known as Lords of the Levee. Both were later elected as aldermen in Chicago's First Ward, the richest but most corrupt ward in Chicago then. It boasted of diverse businesses such as bordellos, cheap hotels, nightclubs, bars, and churches. That meant brothel-keepers, prostitutes, bettors, thieves, businessmen, and professional and common crooks.

The First Ward operated wide open up until around 1910, when all houses of ill repute and betting parlors were forced to close. But that was not the end of the notorious era of Chicago's underworld; it was only a precursor of what followed. During the early years of the mob presence, many notable characters appeared from out of nowhere, including Al Capone, Dion O'Banion, Bugs Moran, and Tony Accardo to name a few.

Around the time of the Great Depression, Chicago underwent numerous changes and considerable turmoil. Chicago was in a for a turbulent ride for years to follow. Many events changed the culture and tone of the city between 1930 and 1939. Chicago held a Century of Progress World's Fair. There were outbreaks of violence by those calling themselves Communists on streets and public property. The University of Chicago Medical Center was completed. The Committee on Social Thought was formed. The Heisman Trophy was awarded for the first time in Chicago in 1937 by the Downtown Athletic Club.

A second Chicago Union Stock Yard fire in Chicago's history happened in 1934.

It was not long until a great migration of blacks from the south settled on the South Side, which later became known as the Black Belt.

The Little Steel Strike, as it was referred to, was an indiscriminate and brutal slaughter of ten people by police. The Chicago Cubs baseball team won the National League pennant.

And Raceway Park was completed.[1]

The underworld that became entrenched during those early years runs deep in Chicago's fabric today. It's not the bad boys of yesteryear but a new breed. They are smart, sophisticated bankers, lawyers, and entrepreneurs along with street thugs who are brilliant and intense in their own right. They are the street-smart pimps, drug dealers, and savvy hustlers experienced in handling the dangers in their urban environment.

Chicago is still as lawless and corrupt as it was earlier but on a diverse

---

[1] Wikipedia. Raceway Park (Illinois) (1938-2000)

level. Its violent, corrupt ways are more intense and unforgiving today as at any time in its past. Today's drive-by shootings and killings in the Windy City are no different than they were in the '20s and '30s, only more frequent and without explanation, purpose, or justification. No matter how much things have changed over the years, violence still runs rampant in Chi-Town. Gang violence and lawlessness are no different from the mob supremacy. There's still an ongoing, uphill battle as the city fathers raise public awareness along with their rage against such acts of violence but to no avail. It's difficult to suppress the taking of life young and old without rhyme or reason.

The new breed began forming in the late 1960s on Chicago's South Side. Two rival groups laid the foundation for a gang called the Black Gangster Disciples. Since that time, numerous gangs have continually reorganized themselves and engage in deadly activity to retain power and dominance over rival gangs. Gangs with diverse backgrounds and ethnicities clash with each other over anything not in their best interests. You find pockets of the new breed in all neighborhoods in Chicago and especially those on the South Side.

The Black Gangster Disciples is one of the most notorious and infamous of all the gangs running wild in the city. Many gang leaders are relocated because of their criminal backgrounds to Illinois correctional facilities or more secure correctional institutions to serve time for their misdeeds.

While incarcerated, the likes of George "Boonie Black" Davis, Roger Cochise Collins, and Maurice King Baldy Jackson founded the Black Gangsters (BG), which pledges its affiliation with the Folk Nation group while still maintaining its ties with the Royal Family. Though not on the streets, they still maintain strong ties with their affiliates on the outside. Small but organized groups in state prisons and other facilities carry on business as usual controlling their own pockets of the drug trade throughout certain neighborhoods.

During the 1980s, some inner-city neighborhoods combined forces with the new breed including the BGs, the Conservative Vice Lords, the Traveling Vice Lords, and the Black Souls thugs to control the drug trade in their respective hoods. The new breeds branched out to other states and grew their following well into the thousands, and they are still growing and active today.

CHAPTER 1

Chicago—Mud City, Chi-Town, Windy City—has been a place of unrest and turmoil from its inception. At one time, the Irish and Italians were the forces to be reckoned with during the mid to late 1800s. Then out of the blue came John "Mush mouth" Johnson, the first black hoodlum with enough clout to muscle his way into a mainly all-white business. Johnson, known as the Policy King, established a saloon and gambling business along with two others, Bill "Dice Man" Lewis and Tom McGinnis. They opened the Frontenac Club on the second floor of a building they owned with Big Jim Colosimo. Johnson's upscale illegal gambling and saloon business catered mostly to wealthy whites in downtown Chicago during the early 1900s. He ran the business with his associates for a short time until his demise in 1907, which was attributed to stress rather than natural causes.

That was the beginning of the end of the reign of Italians and Irish. The next few years, Chi-Town became a mecca for many ethnicities, each with its own rules and code of conduct. With so many groups, there were always differences of opinions and principles. Each faction had its own temperament, which was revealed by its actions and violence.

How Chicago has survived its seemingly unsurmountable obstacles of the past remains a mystery. To this day, it remains resilient enduring countless setbacks, pitfalls, and atrocities as it struggles to recover from its humble beginnings.

In the early 1960s, Chicago went through another metamorphosis; this new revolution of crime and violence has lasted longer than that of the gangsters of yesteryear. A new breed has entrenched its underworld activities more deeply in the Chicago's fabric than any of its predecessors. Chicago, one of the world's most dangerous municipalities with a tarnished reputation synonymous with gang aggression and violence. No matter how hard the city has tried to eradicate the violence, it continues stronger and more vibrant than ever.

The Chicago police has shared part of the city's violent past from its inception by accepting bribes and inducements from different factions. With so much deceit and dishonesty, the city has become embroiled in a virtually impossible task of ridding itself of the undeniable political influence of the drug underworld. Until the city further awakens, this type of behavior will remain and the current mindset of those politicians will continue. Ridding the city of its underlying problems and criminal behavior must begin at the top and trickle down. The dishonest and double-dealing politicians and those appointed to enforce the laws must be held accountable if this problem is to be eradicated. Then and only then will the bulk of the crime problems Chicago faces be removed or eradicated.

CHAPTER 2

Alfonso Lewis, a teenager, had gained a reputation for selling ordinary drugs. It was not until later that potent, mind-altering hallucinogens such as LSD, sometimes referred to as sunshine, became available to street vendors. Alfonso was one of the first in his neighborhood to sell the new drug, and he quickly became known as Sunshine.

Certain drugs have been banned, but they continue to be manufactured in backroom labs throughout the country. They are still available on the black market today and are highly sought after as recreational drugs in some locales. All drugs today consumed by drug addicts are taken orally or injected and are much more potent than drugs of the past.

Sunshine had worked his way up the chain of command to become one of the most successful drug dealers of all time in and around Chicago. During his earlier days selling drugs, he was arrested and charged with several felony counts of distributing illegal drugs. After being brought before the court, he was found guilty on all charges and sent to prison for several years. Sunshine vowed he would never spend time in such a place ever again once he was released.

On a cold, wintery day in late November, Sunshine was released from prison after having served only twelve years of a twenty-year sentence. He was met by one of his homies outside the prison gates, who drove him back to his old haunt on the lower West Side to begin anew. It was his first taste of freedom in over twelve years. Sunshine was eager to return to the hood to resume his unscrupulous lifestyle, the only life he'd ever known.

Back in his sanctuary, he moved back in with his white chick, White

Chocolate. Sunshine had been lucky to meet up with her prior to his imprisonment. She was a gifted leader in her own right and had run the lucrative day-to-day business while he had been incarcerated. She was as tough as they came but fair to the group as they trekked through the daily routine attending to business until Sunshine's return. The street boys, staff, and enforcers on the payroll respected White Chocolate and did their jobs without question. She was one of a kind.

Prior to Sunshine's departure to the big house, their small group had been given the handle the Source. It was associated with the Black Gangster Disciples, who worked the streets of Chicago with impunity at the time of Sunshine's internment. The Source had free rein of the lower southwestern and northeastern part of the city and points in between thanks to the corrupt politicians and police deeply embedded in the system.

With Sunshine's assistance from prison, the Black Gangster Disciples increased its membership tenfold during his absence. After returning and seeing what radical changes had occurred in Chi-Town during his time away, Sunshine decided to reformulate the way the group ran its business. This change had to be done quickly if it was to remain viable. So, he and White Chocolate gathered a large contingent of Disciples and the interim board of directors.

Once the group was assembled in the stash house, Sunshine brought the meeting to order and informed them of the new charter. The new regulations inserted into the charter reinforced the old principles governing the hierarchy of the different sections of the business. He made sure that everyone understood the new guidelines and that each group was on the same page concerning the new rules and guiding principles. He wanted them to understand that the new directives were to be strictly adhered to. If the clique was to survive, its members had to be tight-knit and shrewd; that was the sole purpose of the new rules.

Just as any corporation does when it wishes personnel changes, the Black Disciples held elections after the meeting. Sunshine and several others put their names on the ballot for several open positions in the organization. Sunshine and White Chocolate were the only two running for chairman and cochairman respectively, and they were elected by acclamation.

With full power and control, Sunshine and White Chocolate were able to dictate the group's direction and goals. It was their job to keep the group in line with the help of its newly elected board members. The underlings were to focus on directing the intricate, daily activities of the group. Sunshine had been down that road before, but times had changed drastically while he was incarcerated. The new breeds around Chi-Town had become more forceful, and the streets were more brutal than he remembered. It was not the hood that changed but the attitudes of the new breeds on the streets and their approach to aggression in and outside the neighborhoods.

After all positions in the organization were filled, it was time to get back to doing what they did best—selling drugs. Sunshine immediately began his new role as chairman by contacting distributors for high-grade cocaine, weed, and narcotics.

It was a new ballgame, which included several new gangs coexisting with the Black Disciples. The Latinos, Italians, Asians—each clique had become an entity of fear, and all were fighting for new territory in the city and outlying 'burbs. It was just short of mass hysteria everywhere they looked. Everyone was now armed, locked, and loaded and not hesitant to use firepower at the drop of a hat. When a gang member of one hood ran across a gang member from another hood in or near his territory, more likely than not, a gun battle would erupt—and it did not end there.

The rival invaders of the hood were visited by the competing group, who hunted down the trespassers and assaulted them, which only added fuel to the violence. There was no end in sight to this bloody insanity carried out on the bad streets of Chi-Town daily.

The police had their hands full as gun battles between rival gangs broke out. Drive-by shootings and murders were a daily occurrence. Drug dealers were on every corner with stash houses strategically located throughout neighborhoods. Everywhere you looked in the city and out-lying 'burbs were pushers and addicts.

Police patrolled the mean streets regularly but more often than not with their eyes closed to the open selling of drugs. Drug pushers who were arrested were bailed out and back on the streets within hours. Gang members had no fear of law enforcement and worked the streets selling their merchandise with impunity. It was like living in the Wild West—little or no law and order.

Sunshine regained his rightful position on the West Side along with White Chocolate; he was once again in control of their neighborhood. Not long after being voted in as the chairman of the board, Sunshine and White Chocolate reorganized the operation in their neighborhood and surrounding area. The two ran a tight ship and allowed little if any interference from other hoods. Intrusions by rival gangs were immediately addressed and came with stiff consequences. In prison, Sunshine had learned to be ruthless and unforgiving. He had become hardened and merciless with little or no feelings for his adversaries and didn't tolerate bad behavior from anyone in his organization or those with views or beliefs that differed from his. He was uncompromising.

One morning after conferring with his street boys before they left for the daily grind on the streets, he warned them not to return until they had sold all the drugs in their possession. Some of them had been sluffing off, and he was not going to tolerate that. It was his way or they were out. They quickly got the message.

Not long after the street boys hit the streets that morning, a rival gang came into the neighborhood driving through the area at a high rate of speed and shooting randomly at the street boys and spotters on the street corners. The shootings left one of Sunshine's street boys dead and one wounded. They learned later that morning after some investigating, a group of Latin Kings had been responsible for the drive-by. That was the first real problem Sunshine faced since returning.

The Latin Kings had formed sometime in the early fifties and were still one of the most vicious and notorious groups in Chi-Town. They concentrated mostly in and around the South and West Sides of the city in less-desirable areas. They were the vilest group in Chi-Town at that time; they were very motivated and volatile. With their big number of members, they were considered one of the most ruthless but the most loyal and faithful of all the groups.

Joining the Latin Kings was for life. To be accepted into the group, someone had to go through a ritual of being severely beaten along with other violent acts too horrible to mention to prove his loyalty before being allowed to join the organization as a gangbanger. But once he was in, there was no turning back; the affiliation was forever—one big family protecting and watching over each other. They were one of the most successful and feared groups coast to coast and many municipalities in between.

Sunshine had to retaliate against the Latin Kings on their turf. He vowed to hunt the perpetrators down and take revenge against the offenders before the situation got out of hand. This was a job for the inside group known as the street enforcers, who demanded an eye for an eye. It was not acceptable for any Kings to invade the Disciples' hood without facing severe repercussions.

The Latin Kings' desire was to be the top dog, the top gang in the city, and they were willing to do anything to achieve that status. The Latinos were involved in sexual assault, robbery, murder, mayhem, and selling drugs and paraphernalia. Name it, and if it was illegal, they were involved. The Latinos were a force to be reckoned with, but so was Sunshine.

He gathered his street enforcers after the shooting and told Marcus, his next in command after White Chocolate, what he wanted the enforcers to accomplish—locate those responsible for this violence against the Disciples and bring back as many as they could to face their accuser in the stash house. Sunshine wanted to interrogate them before delivering the punishment he deemed necessary to balance the wrong.

It would be no easy task for Marcus and his enforcers to locate the perpetrators. It was difficult for his small group even to enter the Latinos' territory without being spotted let alone snatch those responsible for this latest tragedy. But something had to be done to quell the situation, and the sooner the better.

Marcus and the other enforcers proceeded to the Latin Kings' realm to begin their search for the intruders. They sank down low in the car and observed the goings on in and around the Latin Kings' neighborhood. Late that afternoon, Marcus's group caught a break. An enforcer spotted what appeared to be the car used in the drive-by. A young Latin King drove past Marcus and his enforcers, unaware of them. The young driver parked just down the street from where Marcus's group was parked. As the young Latin King exited his car, all four of the doors of Marcus's car quickly opened. The street enforcers ran quickly but silently up behind the young Latino, grabbed him, hustled him back to their vehicle, and threw him into the back seat. Two enforcers got on either side of him. Marcus and the other enforcers jumped in, slammed their doors, and headed back to the stash house.

Marcus parked behind it where they could not be seen from the street. The young Latino hostage was physically removed from the back seat and hustled up the back steps, through the back door, and down into the basement, where he was shackled to an iron ring attached to the wall that was high up enough that the Latino had to stand. Marcus left the remaining enforcers to watch the detainee; he needed to inform Sunshine.

Sunshine was in his small office when Marcus appeared at the door. "We apprehended one of the Latinos responsible for the assassination. He's shackled in the basement."

"Take a seat, Marcus. Tell me about it."

"We went to the Latin Kings' hood and waited most of the day in the car when by chance a car fitting the description drove by driven by the same young Latino King who was spotted during the drive-by. He must have been blind not to see us as he passed. He parked only a couple of spaces away from us. We grabbed him as he was getting out of his car without being spotted. We'd been sitting in that spot since early morning and were ready to call it a day when suddenly he appeared out of nowhere. I'm sure he was one of the ones involved in the killing of Joe-Joe and the wounding of Fats. Hopefully, after we give him a taste of what he did to those two, he'll tell us the identity of the others involved that day. Maybe after we learn their identities, we'll be able to hunt them down one by one and give them their just dues."

Sunshine thought they had been lucky not to be spotted as they sat on the street for the biggest part of the day. If they had been identified, it could have been a totally different outcome. It had been a perfectly executed seizure and would be talked about for days to come in the stash house.

"Good, Marcus. Let's see if we can get him to confess and name some sorry-ass names."

They headed to the basement, where the young Latin King was dangling from the O-ring. Sunshine looked directly into the young Latin King's penetrating, hostile, dark eyes. "I'm here to learn who was with you in the car that day when without provocation you gunned down two of my street boys. Do I make myself clear? If you tell me, we can get this over quickly. If not, you know the drill."

The Latino glared at Sunshine without blinking. "I no squealin' on or involve any of my homeboys. Ju and jour gang can go to hell as far as I concerned. Jou get nothin' from me!"

"If that's the way you want to play, get ready to meet your maker." Sunshine saw the young Latino's eyes fill with horror.

Sunshine told Marcus, "It's up to you and your enforcers to find out who the others were. When you find out, come tell me."

Sunshine went upstairs. Marcus and two of his henchmen remained in the basement. Marcus approached the young Latino to find out who else was in the car for the drive-by. Marcus's demeanor escalated quickly until he was in a rage. He mercilessly beat and questioned the young man, but he realized that the Latino was not going to implicate anyone or divulge any information. Marcus relented. The beating had been for nothing. The young Latino was as tough as they came. The Latino said nothing, He didn't even whimper despite the pain he endured. It was not pleasant even for Marcus or his assistants to witness such acts of viciousness on such a young person. Even though he was partly responsible for the taking of a life, he showed no sign of regret or remorse. A tough hombre to be sure, one of kind, someone you might run into once in a lifetime.

"That's enough for now," Marcus announced. "We'll return later and finish what we started." Marcus headed to Sunshine's office and told him, "Can't get a thing outta him. The beating didn't work. I don't know what else me and my boys can do to extract information from him. He's not giving it up."

"Let's give him a reprieve, Marcus. Go back later and see if he's had a change of heart."

Later that evening, after giving the young Latino time to recoup, Marcus and his two henchmen returned to the basement. The Latino's head was bowed. Blood dripping from his broken nose drying in a puddle on the basement floor. Marcus began his questioning and physical punishment again; this time, the punishment was harsher involving different methods of persuasion—a baseball bat, a hot poker in and around the genital areas—and it was not long until the young Latino passed out. At that point, the young Latino was not going to divulge anything to anyone. They left him hanging from the ring.

The following morning, Marcus and Sunshine returned to the basement. The unresponsive Latino looked as if he had been run through a wringer. He was bloody from head to toe; his color had turned ashen. He died over night without divulging or revealing any association connected to the incident. He was as hardcore as they came.

"Marcus, you and two of your subordinates drag his sorry ass out to the car and dump him where you picked him up. The Latin Kings will know who did this. It'll remind them that we won't tolerate what they did, that they shouldn't screw with us. An eye for an eye in any language is tough revenge."

Marcus, returned to the basement, along with his henchmen removed the unresponsive Latino from the O-ring and carried him out to the car. They drove back where they abducted him, and looked around. The streets were empty—no visible signs of Latino gang activity. Marcus stopped in the middle of the street, and two of the enforcers pushed the body of the Latino out of the car and onto the street and drove away.

A day later, Sunshine read an article in the paper entitled "Young Latino Boy Found Dead on the South Side." The article stated, "The body of a young Latino was found in the street near the corner of North Broadway and Wilson Avenue yesterday morning around seven thirty … Anyone with information concerning this matter is requested to contact the police immediately." Sunshine knew repercussions from the Latin Kings were now unavoidable, but as of now, the score was even. Tit for tat.

Sunshine told Marcus, "The police discovered that Latino boy's body in the street where you dumped it yesterday morning. They have no evidence yet as to how he died or who may have been responsible. The paper stated the coroner would determine the cause of death and his findings would be forthcoming.

The paper indicated the police believes it's gang related, so we need to lie low for a while and stay out of Latin Kings territory."

"I'm sure the Latin Kings knew it was in retaliation for their killing and injuring two of ours, but I'm sure they'll keep it quiet," Marcus replied.

The newspaper also stated, "The police had several avenues to consider, but they consider it to be gang related. It could more than likely turn into another unsolved case like so many other cases in Chicago. This could be another travesty of justice never to be resolved."

Sunshine indicated to Marcus, "Keep a close lookout for any reprisals. I'm sure the Latin Kings are chomping at the bit to even the score, so be careful."

CHAPTER 3

Sunshine and his organization began encroaching on small pockets of drug-infested areas in and around the neighborhood searching for wannabes, local groups willing to hook up with the BGD or too small to resist a takeover. The gang was increasing in size and clout on the West Side and in a few smaller pockets throughout the South Side of the city.

Since their last run-in with the Latin Kings, things had returned to some semblance of order. No one on the West Side or South Side was assaulting other groups trying to muscle in. Apparently, the Latin Kings had learned a tough lesson and were staying close to home.

During this latest lull on the West and South sides, the majority of Chicago's gangs were still engaged in drive-bys or other forms of violence on a daily basis. The drug war in the city was raging out of control and as dangerous and treacherous as ever. It was reported in the papers that crime of every description was on the rise and showing no signs of ending anytime soon.

The Asians were growing by leaps and bounds with new recruits entering the city weekly. The Italians were still in the mix but not as strong or as respected as in the past. It was getting harder and harder for the Italians to go about business as usual as they clashed with the new groups popping up all around the city.

The Latino gangs with a large influx of illegals from south of the border were becoming more powerful in New York, Texas, and Florida as well as Chicago.

The drug trade more profitable than ever, as the availability of new drugs was on the rise. A hefty increase in the number of drug addicts adding to the mix made it even more desirable. Drug zones in each section of the country were fighting to keep territory they controlled, and no one gave an inch. Daily drive-bys, murders, corruption, and prostitution were the norm in most large cities. The police were limited in their capabilities to fight the growing violence and chaos.

Sunshine and his posse of misfits, nonconformist, renegades, drop-outs, and bad boys gained stature during this period and earned the respect of other gangs as they spread throughout neighborhoods in and around the West and Southwest Sides of Chicago. Sunshine was all business and well respected; he had earned a reputation as a straight shooter. Any BGD who ran into trouble sought him out to solve his problem. Sunshine became a powerhouse no one wanted to be on the wrong side of.

One afternoon, Sunshine was making a large purchase of cocaine, opioids, marijuana, and ecstasy from one of the largest suppliers in the area. The final price the dealer quoted was exceedingly high. Sunshine, believing the dealer was trying to price him out of the business, told him, "I'm taking my business elsewhere."

This of course angered the dealer, told Sunshine, "Sorry you feel that way. Don't darken my doorstep again. You've just locked yourself out."

Sunshine had stored away extra amounts of drugs for just such a scenario; he could operate for a couple of weeks or until he could find a new supplier. Shortly thereafter, while having lunch with a group of friends at a local café, he was introduced to Slice, a New Yorker who was a distributor for a large drug group on the East Coast. Slice before leaving, told Sunshine, "If you're ever in need of a supplier, and I can be of assistance, don't hesitate to get in touch with me."

After Slice left, Sunshine told the others, "I'd like to meet with this Slice again while he's still in town. Can anyone here arrange a meeting?"

"You bet," one local member said. "I'll set up an appointment for you with him."

"I appreciate that. I'll owe you one."

Later that day, Sunshine's phone rang. The one who said he would arrange the meeting said, "Slice is willing to meet with you tomorrow morning before he leaves."

The next day, Sunshine met with Slice to discuss the drugs Slice could supply. Slice was impressed with the way Sunshine approached his business dealings and casually mentioned to Sunshine, "We have an affiliation with the infamous Gangster Crips. Have you heard of them?"

"Who hasn't? I've always been impressed with their organization."

"Would you be interested becoming a supplier and dealer for the Chicago area?"

Sunshine was stunned; Slice had just asked him to become a wholesale supplier with one of the largest suppliers in the country, something Sunshine had had in mind since getting out of prison, but he did not have an in with any of the large dealers. The ultimate reward in the drug business was becoming a wholesale supplier. He was excited at the thought and accepted his offer. He knew this would cause him trouble with the local suppliers, but he was willing to take that risk.

Slice, wanting to expand his territory in the Midwest and especially in Chi-Town, took Sunshine into his confidence and told him that he could supply him whatever drugs he needed. That meant Sunshine would not have to depend on local distributors and their exorbitant prices and uncouth sales tactics. It was a dog-eat-dog business, survival of the fittest, with such unscrupulous, small-time suppliers.

After settling on a price for the drugs he required and the percentage of the profit to be paid to the New York syndicate for setting him up as a supplier, Sunshine was ready to take the plunge. His new provider was able to sell him all the marijuana, opioids, heroin, cocaine, and mollies he required. There were still some hallucinogenic drugs popular in the Chicago area that Slice didn't have access to, but he told Sunshine, "I'll call around and see if I can locate a local source for those drugs. If and when I find a place, I'll order them and inform you."

"Great. Until then, I'm sure I can survive with what you supply me with. I appreciate all you're doing for me, and look forward to doing business with you and your organization."

"Sunshine, if you run into any trouble and I can be of help, call me, here's my card. Your well-being is my concern now. I want things to run smoothly for our mutual benefit. Know where I'm coming from?"

"Yes."

"Keep in touch."

Slice left, and Sunshine returned to his stash house to await his order from New York. It took only a couple of days before a courier delivered several packages from New York. Once the packages were signed for and brought into the house, Sunshine put his grunts to work cutting and packaging the drugs. Except for the benzodiazepine, methamphetamine, and a couple of other drugs he normally handled, the supply from New York was enough for him to get by with until a new channel of distribution could be located for the remaining drugs.

Soon, business was humming along with no interference from the local authorities, drug pushers or suppliers, or drive-bys. Things in the neighborhood had settled down, and the drug business had become more lucrative than ever; Sunshine was not only selling drugs on the streets but was also acting as a local supplier. The money was coming in faster than he had anticipated. Business was flourishing.

It was not long before several of the smaller supplier/dealers became upset with Sunshine and his new operation. The Latin Kings and Asians began aggressively intimidating his street boys and street soldiers, harassing them by selling drugs in and around his neighborhood and undercutting his prices. Sunshine decided to strike back with an all-out turf war. Violence on the West Side increased drastically. Distressing as it was, it did not last long. Too many were getting killed or injured while others fled the area in fear for their lives.

The police became involved in this latest debacle and began patrolling the streets in force, arresting and booking anyone caught loitering. The police with their informants and snitches helped law enforcement root out certain undesirables. It was not long until the violence was quelled and gang activity returned to a controllable level. The turf war was at a standstill. The factions quietly returned to business as usual.

White Chocolate came into Sunshine's office one morning with a huge black eye. Sunshine was taken aback at the sight. "What the hell happened to you? Run into a door?"

"No. Wish it was that simple. I was on my way to deliver one of the street boys a message when someone came up from behind and waylaid me with a sucker punch. I screamed and got Junior's attention. He was standing across the street."

"Did you recognize who did this to you?"

"No, but when Junior ran over to help, the Latino split. We saw him turn the corner, hop into a waiting car, and drive off."

"Did Junior recognize the Latino?"

"No, only that he appeared to be a Latino from the East Side."

"How did Junior know that?"

"He recognized a tattoo on the guy's left hand, a five-pointed star. And wearing the gang colors."

"At least he's not a West or South Side Latino gangbanger. I'll find the scumbag and burn his sorry ass. You want to go to the emergency room?"

"No, I'm fine. Don't worry about me. I've had worse injuries learning jiu-jitsu, ha! But his attack was so fast that I didn't have time to defend myself. I sure didn't see it coming."

"If you ever see this scumbag again, let me or one of the boys know. I'll give this SOB a taste of his own medicine, and it won't be something he'll forget. I'm sure he's hightailed it out of the area by now, but I'll have the boys ask around the neighborhood in case he's still lurking around out there. Keep your eyes open when you go out alone like that. You never know who you'll run into." Sunshine whispered.

White Chocolate left to run daily errands, which was part of her daily activities. She was in charge of supplies, food, paying the bills, and keeping a roster concerning obligations of the street boys and those in the stash house. She was an integral part of the business and knew more about its workings than Sunshine. She had maintained the fledgling business while Sunshine was away in prison. She had become as knowledgeable and as tough as anyone in the business.

White Chocolate, a player whom the rest of the group looked up to and respected unequivocally. Sunshine was fortunate having such a devoted partner working with him, one whom he could trust explicitly. Without White Chocolate, he would have been a boat in uncharted waters aimlessly drifting about with currents carrying it to unknown destinations. She had held the organization together with her spunk and determination to be the best no matter the circumstances. She was as tough as they came, but she had a softer side she shared with Sunshine.

CHAPTER 4

One day while talking to one of his customers from the neighborhood, Sunshine learned of a house for sale better suited for his operation than the one he occupied at present and used as a stash house. He asked his customer for the address and phone number, and later that afternoon, he called the owner to inquire about the property. He made arrangements to meet with the owner after work to look at the house.

He and White Chocolate met with the owner, who showed them around the place and the property. They were impressed with the location and the condition of the house and property, and they told the owner, "We're pleased with the place. We need a moment alone to discuss the possibilities and the potential of the property. If we agree it has the basics for our needs, it's definitely something we'd be interested in if we can agree on a price."

"Take your time. I'm in no rush this evening. My wife and kids are at a school function."

Sunshine and White Chocolate walked outside to discuss the property. They agreed it met their needs. They went back inside and told the owner, "We like the location, and it's perfect for what we have in mind. I want to make you an offer you can't refuse."

"If I decide to sell the property to you, I want cash up front, no checks or contracts."

"Fair enough," Sunshine said. He offered him a price that he readily accepted.

Sunshine told him, "My partner or I will return tomorrow with the cash so we can get started with the paperwork. We need to remodel and renovate before moving in."

The next few days were hectic with running the business and trying to get the paperwork completed and house transferred into White Chocolate's name. Putting her name on the deed would not draw as much attention as would putting Sunshine's name on it. His being a convicted felon might have raised some unnecessary red flags. The sale in general went smoothly with only a couple of hiccups, and within two weeks, they were ready to do minor remodeling and renovations. After the work was accomplished, they were ready to move into their new location.

It did not take long before they were open for business in the new neighborhood. The only potential problem was that the house was closer to the Latin Kings' turf than they anticipated. This was a new wrinkle for the Source; they would have to do conduct business closer to the Latin Kings working the nearby streets.

It did not take long before skirmishes arose along the invisible boundaries separating the different blocks in the same area. Something had to be done fast or the BGD would lose what territories they had established in and around the West and South Sides. Sunshine contacted a couple of dealers in the area whom he was having disputes with and offered them a deal to join forces. At first, they were skeptical, but as time passed, they came to the realization that it was in their best interests. In the end, they joined forces with the BGD, and eventually, the groups expanded and covered almost a fourth of the territory on the West and South Sides and business boomed. The Source was becoming a force to be reckoned with on the West and South Sides of the city.

In due course, Sunshine permitted the different groups to take back their streets; all the while, he was becoming more and more influential not only as a street vendor but also as a wholesaler. He continued to gain influence and prestige throughout the West Side with the help of White Chocolate, who had become somewhat of a pillar of the community. Money flowed in so fast that they had little time to count it, let alone spend it.

Not long after, White Chocolate told Sunshine, "I've talked to a number of locals and several community leaders and learned many families in the area are strapped for cash. What do you say about paying some of their overdue bills and real estate taxes and supplying those most venerable with food? We'll not flaunt what we're doing but quietly go about helping some of the neighbors out by lifting that burden so they can get back on their feet."

White Chocolate convinced Sunshine also to revitalize the large park in the neighborhood and give the young people and residents somewhere to relax and play during the summer. She was taking on a lot of projects that had been ignored over time; she was elated about doing something good for those around her. Besides running the stash house, she became an ambassador of sorts for the neighborhood. By manipulating and laundering the dirty money they made selling drugs, White Chocolate anonymously donated a large portion of it to several projects. A few locals knew who was behind the scenes and sponsoring those projects in the neighborhood, but would never divulge who it was.

Her hard work in the neighborhood and what she accomplished did not go unnoticed. Within two years of revitalizing certain projects on the West and South Sides of the city, she captured the attention of several local officials. White Chocolate eventually was recognized for her civic work restoring the park, which was eventually renamed in her honor.

Sunshine became less involved in selling on the streets to druggies leaving that once again to White Chocolate and gang members; while he became the go-to person for large dealers throughout the Chicago area. Sunshine's distribution business continued to grow and flourish, and somehow able in staying out of the limelight. He was a shrewd, cautious businessman who was able to avoid conflict with city officials and local police. The drug money had been spent wisely, and in time, he too became known by the local officials appreciating the good he and White Chocolate were doing for the West and South Side.

He could still be a tyrant when required, but overall, he had earned the community's and the dealers' respect and accepted. He no longer had a bad-boy reputation or persona around the neighborhood or with those in high places in the inner city. Eventually, he earned the respect of the local gangbangers, who stopped hassling him and his organization. As long as most traffickers, drug pushers, and gangbangers knew where he was and what he was doing, they pretty much left him alone. He paid his dues, but there were still those whom he paid off enabling him to continue business as usual. They were the diehard local consortiums and those with influence and certain authority within the system.

Since Sunshine and White Chocolate became so vigilant at running their business, it was scary even to them at times. They knew it was only a matter of time until their bubble burst and things once again headed south. They were realistic about that aspect of the business.

One day out of the blue, Chicago flipped upside down; everything became chaotic. Bedlam reigned. They hit rock bottom. All good things come to an end, and the end came without warning.

The competition, bad blood between rival gangs had been growing exponentially. In the previous few months and years, it had become impossible to do business without stepping on someone's toes.

As times changed, so did the gangs' needs. They became greedier and started reverting to the violent, dog-eat-dog, shoot or be shot, take no prisoners was the latest status quo. Looting, murder, robbery, rape, and arson were running rampant once again on the West and South Side, and throughout the inner city. City officials and law enforcement agencies were unable to stem the tide and amount of lawlessness throughout the area. The whole city was out of control.

The mayor and the governor met to decide what to do to quell the unlawful and criminal activity strangling the city. They had no choice but to involve the local national guard; they needed more boots on the ground to free up the police in order to do their job. The extra manpower would help stem the violence and hopefully return the town to some semblance of order.

Until this lunacy between rival gangs and different factions struggling for power was eradicated, the city could not or would not function properly. This insanity had to end and quickly if the city was to survive the upheaval and bedlam of this latest outbreak.

That was not the first time this type of behavior had shown its ugly self in Chi-Town and more than likely not be the last. Chicago, a city with a reputation of disorder and mayhem since its inception in the 1830s, always seemed to find a way to survive.

As the national guard troops took up positions throughout the city, the mayhem began slowly decreasing day after day until finally it was squelched. Its return to some sense of order was a big step in the right direction for enforcement agencies.

The drug trafficking had not been completely immobilized, but the bedlam tearing the city apart had been suppressed at least for the moment. It was once again peaceful around the city; with most of the violence suppressed. There were still small pockets of violence erupting occasionally, but quickly curbed by the police.

During this time, Sunshine's business diminished. Getting supplies from out of town to sell and stay afloat in his ever-changing world was difficult. The hardest thing for him was to get used to being less and less a player in this new era of gangbanging. The new gangs were more powerful and forbidding. They brought their own set of rules to town.

The Mexicans, Latinos, Asians, Russians, and Italians each worked out of their own playbooks each with their rules for doing business and handling violence. It had become a difficult place to do business. Unlike most other businesses, the drug business was in a league of its own. A killer instinct was required to run such a business and not become a nonplayer in this horrific game, survival of the fittest. Sunshine was pushed to the brink of disaster before finally deciding to get back in the game bigger, better, and more powerful than ever.

On a cold winter morning in 1988, he made his move. He amassed a small army of thugs, bullies, and hardcore criminals and ordered them to take over neighborhoods one street at a time to reclaim BGD former territory and status. They quickly got back in the swing of things. Once he set his mind to do something, Sunshine didn't stop until he reached his goal. He aggressively battled rival gangs, which were stunned by the way he went about his daily activities.

As the time passed, gangs throughout Chi-Town saw the handwriting on the wall and relinquished certain territories back to the BGD. It was not long before he once again was the most feared and dreaded drug lord in the city; he regained his status among the cutthroat gangs as the most powerful drug lord around, and was merciless when it came to conducting business. His group when cut loose was not one to tangle with or go up against in any way. Those who pushed back on the BGD were shown no mercy. Even local authorities were frightened of him and his rough group of hellions. BGD again had the run of the whole West and South Side. He was back on the scene with a vengeance.

White Chocolate in the meantime became pregnant, which did not sit well with Sunshine. His plate was full; the last thing he needed was more confusion and complications. He told her that she should take time off to care for herself and the baby, that she did not need to be around all the upheaval of the business and drugs, which could possibly cause problems with the baby.

White Chocolate was mildly upset with his suggestion but knew better than to cause a scene. She knew that when he set his mind to something, he did not bend. She decided to stay home until the baby arrived. It was a big letdown for her, but she knew it was in the best interests of Sunshine, her, and the baby. She told him, "I'll be going home this evening and I'll not return until after the delivery. If you need my assistance during my absence, just call me."

"Yes, I know. I also know I want only the best for you and the baby. I have a lot on my mind right now and don't need more distractions. I'm sure you most of all understand that."

"Yes, I understand. I'll be fine. It's just that I'll miss the interaction here at the stash house with you and the boys."

"Why don't you find someone to help you during the day to run the house?"

"That's an idea, but I don't think I need anyone right now. Maybe later, I'll find someone to help me clean, cook, and run errands during the latter stages of my pregnancy. Maybe even keep them around for a while after I return home with the baby. Until then, I'll manage the household chores myself. I'm going to miss you, but I know it's for the best."

"I'll be home every night to make sure you and the baby are looked after. I can even pick up suppers on my way home so you don't have to cook. You're all the family I have. I don't want anything to happen to you or our baby."

White Chocolate left the stash house thinking it would be difficult for her since she had been such a major player in the gang for half her life. She felt alone not knowing what the future held for her. She was leaving her stash house family. Her thoughts were mixed as she thought about her pregnancy and her new role as a mother. After she gave birth and things settled down around the house, she would return to work stronger than ever and be Sunshine's right hand again.

Sunshine knew her absence would be a hardship on the business as well. She had become more of a partner than a lover; she had been his Rock of Gibraltar. She knew as much about if not more than he did about the business. She was the cornerstone of the organization. It was going to be different around the stash house without her charm and guidance. But the stress in the stash house had taxed them both; he didn't need any more distraction, but he would miss her help.

She told those in the stash house that she would be leaving until the baby arrived. Everyone told her she'd be sorely missed, and wished her well. Once outside the stash house, she let out a big sigh, climbed into her car and drove away, not looking back. She was no longer a player. It had been a rewarding journey she'd been on for the previous several years. It would take time for her to settle down into her new role as housewife and mother. *Life is not always fair,* she thought as she headed home. But it didn't take her long to realize Sunshine had been right to ask her to spend time getting things ready for their new arrival.

CHAPTER 5

The next morning as Sunshine was heading off to work, said good-bye to White Chocolate, who felt apprehensive about being left alone. Becoming a mother meant leaving the team behind and contemplating motherhood. She was nervous about the whole situation she found herself in, but knew it would be an exciting journey once the baby arrived.

Sunshine felt a void when he arrived at the stash house that morning. Without White Chocolate, the stash house seemed empty. It would take time for him and the gang members to adjust to not having her around. She had been the adhesive holding this group of misfits together. She had been the go-to person with those who had a problem. She wore many hats as she tended to her part of the business while Sunshine did his manly thing.

Sunshine had to step up to the plate if he was to run the organization without White Chocolate's assistance. New challenges presented themselves; he had to manage new curves, bends, and twists in the road ahead while hitting the ground running. But he quickly learned that that was not as easy as he had contemplated earlier. Quickly becoming overwhelmed trying to handle all that she had handled, that which he had always taken for granted. She had accomplished her work effortlessly, seemingly behind the scenes. She would be sorely missed by everyone at the house especially Sunshine.

Her first day at home alone, White Chocolate began her new role as a soon-to-be mom, but thoughts of what needed to be accomplished at the stash house were still foremost in her mind. She realized she had to stop worrying about how the boys and Sunshine were coping without her presence. She profoundly missed the camaraderie, and worried how Sunshine would manage his new role, but knew that was something she had to overcome and move on.

It was quiet in the house, wondered what she should do first. It certainly was not the hustle and bustle of the stash house she'd grown so accustomed to. She knew she had to get her act together and get started with her new role.

She started by cleaning and dusting the furniture, just to have something to do and clear her mind of thoughts of the stash house. But soon found herself worrying about what her life would be like before and after the baby's arrival. Having no mothering skills, wondered if she would be able to take on the responsibility of a newborn. Would she be able to return to work at the stash house part time during the interim? Her thoughts were running wild with questions she had never considered before. But as the day progressed, she began to regroup; she decided to make the best of her new situation.

Things were getting dicey at the stash house. Sunshine, overwhelmed by the extra work he inherited from White Chocolate, jumped in with both feet and adjusted quickly to his new situation. But nothing was the same without White Chocolate.

He first rearranged the gang members' work schedules. He found himself handling petty grievances of the posse taking him away from more-important work needing his attention. Things went south during his first few hours that first day. So many things were brought to his attention he had no concept of how to deal with, especially certain aspects of running the business. He found it tough to handle the many complications, glitches, and problems within the organization. He struggled through the first half of the day reeling in confusion.

Sunshine was glad to leave the stash house as he headed off to lunch. He hoped some time away from the bedlam would allow him to clear his congested mindset. He drove to a new restaurant a few blocks away from the stash house and as he walked in, saw a couple of rival gang members from the neighboring area staring intensely at him as he walked over to an empty table. He felt the tension. He was by himself and didn't need this aggravation. He wondered what else could happen to further complicate his already complicated day.

After ordering a drink and his lunch, out of the corner of his eye, he noticed the two Latino boys heading toward him. He knew it was not going to be a social call. One Latino leaned over on his table, looked coldly at Sunshine, and said, "You need to leave if you know what's good for you. You're not welcome here old man. It's not your hood or territory, so I suggest you get the f——k out of here and don't return."

Sunshine stood and glared at the two Latino punks. "Back off, a— holes, and get the f——k out of my face!"

One boy reached inside his waist and pulled out a Glock; he pulled the cocking mechanism back and held the gun down by his side.

Sunshine told him, "You better think twice before you do something you'll regret for the rest of your life. Do I make myself clear?" He stared down the two young wannabes.

"You don't scare me, you m——f——er," said the individual closer to Sunshine.

In one fluid motion, Sunshine kicked the table into the Latino hold-ing the weapon taking the petty wannabe by surprise and knocking the gun from his hand as he fell backward onto the floor.

The other gang member backed off the table and went for his weapon hidden beneath his long shirt in his waistband. Sunshine punched him with a haymaker knocking out one of his front teeth and sending him careening over a nearby table and chairs, where he fell with a thud. He lay there motionless.

The other gangbanger on the floor reached for his weapon, which was knocked from his hand as he fell to the floor. It was still a couple of feet from him on the floor when suddenly Sunshine moved quickly around the table and kicked the gun away from his outstretched hand.

"Pick up your compadre and get the f——k out of here before I cause you more embarrassment. Capiche, a—hole?"

The two Latinos got off the floor quickly exited the restaurant. Sunshine sat back down at his table and waited for his lunch. When the waitress arrived with his order, he told her, "I apologize for causing a scene. If I owe anything extra, just add it to my bill."

"Apology accepted. Enjoy your lunch."

His appetite was less than when he ordered, but ate the lunch anyway. He left a larger tip than normal and walked out. He looked around for the two wannabees thinking they could be waiting around some corner to ambush him. Luckily, they were nowhere to be seen. Climbed back into his car and drove straight back to the stash house.

After arriving back inside the stash house, told the others what happened and said that they should keep an eye out for trouble on the streets. They needed to avoid trouble at all costs especially the Latino gangs. Sunshine knew things could change quickly since his altercation with the two wannabees.

That same afternoon, several Latinos were spotted in and around the neighborhood and appeared to be looking for trouble. The next morning, several Latino gangbangers were spotted roaming the neighborhood in small groups presumably after learning what had occurred at the restaurant. They were looking for revenge. Sunshine sent Marcus and his street patrol to try to stop the situation from getting out of control.

The Latinos were advancing farther and farther into the Source's neighborhood; things started to become unglued. Marcus and his street patrol soon came face to face with one of the small gangs in an alley behind a warehouse; they hurled derogatory and offensive verbal abuses at each other, which escalated quickly into brawling and rapidly spiraled out of control. Soon, they engaged in hand-to-hand combat. Shots were fired. Both sides regrouped as the gun battle began raging; it lasted for a couple of minutes. Several Latinos received minor injuries, and one was shot in the leg. Marcus's gang suffered only minor injuries; none had been shot.

The police arrived soon after the incident ended. By that time, all the gangbangers had split. The police canvassed the neighborhood and searched for signs of mayhem and chaos. Finished with their preliminary investigation a few hours later, left the scene. Police had done an extensive search of the area and exhausted their physical and mental resources relating to the activity that occurred earlier. As so often happens in situations like this, the police came up empty-handed. As investigations go, no two people saw or heard the same thing, and difficult piecing together evidence and deciding on who to believe. Another cold case in the making

Having a good idea of who the troublemakers were after questioning local confidential informers (CIs) but without actual proof or positive identification, the police dropped the investigation and chalked it up as another violent, gang-related incident. It wasn't the first, and it would not be the last they were sure. The city files were full of such unresolved cases.

Occasionally, something would trigger a revisit to certain files, and if they were lucky, maybe the police would discover that the MO (modus operandi) of one of the cold cases was the same MO of someone they were working. Sometimes, they were lucky enough to solve both cases, but that was the exception.

CHAPTER 6

After that, things settled down between the Latinos and the Source; it was back to business as usual. The drug trade in and around Cook County was back to doing what it did best, and money was coming in so fast that Sunshine and White Chocolate were running out of places in the stash house to hide the cash. They decided to find a bank outside the US to launder it. They decided to find a bank in the Caymans and take a vacation while there as well.

They flew to the Grand Cayman Island and found a bank willing to accept a large amount cash without question. They opened an account under a pseudonym name plus a seven-digit number in case it was needed. They were told any time they had large sums to deposit or withdraw, all they had to do was fly back to the Caymans or call ahead and give either the seven-digit number or pseudonym listed on the account and the money would be electronically sent to the bank of their choice in the states.

After depositing a large sum of money in the local island bank, decided to take advantage of what the island had to offer. They stayed at a hotel near the waterfront for a few days. This was their first vacation ever while cohabitating. They took in the sights and sounds the island had to offer including the sun, the nightlife, and the restaurants. The money they had accumulated allowed them to take advantage of things unattainable by the average Joe.

They enjoyed their spacious suite in a four-star hotel across the street from the beach. It was nice sitting on the balcony relaxing while looking at the beautiful turquoise water of the gulf and enjoying their riches. It did not them long to realize that this lifestyle was addictive. They were free of their worries and cares in Chicago for a few days; while savoring the moment.

This trip had opened their eyes to the real world, one that operated strictly on cash. Those without it, they learned, were nobodies while those with it were kings and queens. They indulged in their newfound independence and played it to the hilt; they could afford it.

They went to the beach across the street, where they took an underwater sightseeing tour aboard a submersible, a type of submarine, and see what was denoted on the bulletin board as the Wall. This piqued White Chocolate's interest but not Sunshine's; however, she talked him into going along. It was an exciting adventure for White Chocolate, but Sunshine felt extremely claustrophobic in the submersible. Feeling nauseous, light-headed after the hatches were closed reminded him of his prison cell. That was not the highlight of the trip for him by any stretch of the imagination.

White Chocolate was just the opposite; enjoyed the thrill of being in the cramped quarters and witnessing the magnificent, magical underwater world as advertised. She was lured by the unknown.

Once the hatches were closed, sealing out the rest of the word, the next half hour or so, all those aboard packed in this tin can like sardines and several meters below the water's surface looking through portholes at the different marine life living in this enchanted coral wonderland.

The submersible reached its diving depth and made its way in and out of the coral toward the Wall. As the electric submarine proceeded slowly along the bottom, those aboard were amazed as they watched the landscape below suddenly disappear. The submersible had ventured over a sheer drop-off; the sea floor vanished. Things below the sub became pitch-black. White Chocolate had no words to describe her awe. Her heart was racing. She knew she would talk about that experience for years to come.

Sunshine, however, kept his eyes forward. Not once did he take even a quick look at the beauty and tranquility outside the sub. He was terrified and couldn't wait to get back on dry land.

After surfacing, he was barely able to climb out of the submarine. Sunshine, still reeling from the experience, told White Chocolate, "I've experienced that once and that was one too many times. Never again."

She smiled and kissed him. "I admire your courage in taking the trip with me."

After he regained his facilities and land legs, he spotted a beach bar; he wanted to recoup from his harrowing experience and have a casual lunch and stiff drink. They walked into the beach bar and found a table. He needed to unwind and relax. They people-watched as they enjoyed a well-deserved lunch.

Sunshine said, "After lunch, I'd like to try something more my speed. Let's take that glass-bottomed boat ride next." He said with a smirk on his face.

"Sounds great, but do you think you can handle it?" She asked playfully.

"Yes. At least it's not enclosed like the submersible." He chuckled. "And if I want off, I can always jump out of the boat and swim to shore. I can swim but not breathe underwater." Once again chuckling to himself.

After their leisure lunch, they strolled down the beach to the glass bottom boat ride pavilion. The glass bottom boat soon filled with passengers and soon ventured out into the bay; cruising around the small bay weaving in and around tourists snorkeling, taking scuba-diving lessons, or just frolicking in the warm waters near the shore. There was something for everyone in this tropical paradise to enjoy.

Sunshine didn't feel confined in the glass bottom boat. After half an hour or so of viewing varieties of fishes, stingrays, and turtles below in the clear blue water of the bay, the boat returned to the dock, where a new group was already lined up waiting for the next ride. Sunshine and White Chocolate were ready to return to the hotel and take a break from all the hustle and bustle of the day's activities and relax before venturing out later.

White Chocolate asked the concierge after returning to the hotel about a trip to a farm she read about in one of the brochures she picked up after arriving. She and Sunshine had never seen a real farm let alone visited one. She thought it would be a new experience taking a tour of a farm especially on horseback, something neither had experienced. The excursion also boasted of a cave the farm owner recently discovered. The brochure said the cave had several ancient Indian artifacts that had remained undisturbed for centuries.

The concierge made arrangements for the Lewies's to take the tour the following day. They were looking forward to a new adventure. Sunshine looked forward riding a horse most of all. He visualized himself sitting tall in the saddle like John Wayne and riding off into the sunset with the damsel. Both looked forward to exploring part of the Caymans' history. So far, their trip had been the most memorable time of their lives as individuals and as a couple.

They arrived in their suite totally exhausted. They needed a nap before freshening up and heading out later for dinner. There were lots to do on the tiny island, and they wanted to do as much as they could during the short time they were here.

The island had a variety of eating and drinking establishments for the night crowd. Dancing was always on the menu along with the gaiety of musical ensembles. And there was always the late-night walk on the beach.

After taking time to rest and relax, it was time to get up and get ready to hit the strip, time to enjoy the night life the Caymans had to offer. Leaving the hotel, a little early, enjoyed an hour or so of shopping, while moseying through several small stores and gift shops along the beachfront. Each store offered a variety of knickknacks from sunglasses to souvenir T-shirts and a million other inexpensive items from around the world.

It had been a while since they enjoyed themselves at that level, and they were going to make the best of it. They wanted to spread their wings and get down.

Outside, they could hear the music as it began ramping up, up and down the beach; musicians were tuning their instruments getting ready for the influx of tourists and locals for the evening onslaught. Steel drums, guitars, bongos, marimbas, and guiros could be heard as tourist and locals gathered along the crowded sidewalks heading to their favorite watering hole along the beach.

The beach scene was festive and exciting. People crowded into the clubs like sardines just as they were in the Chicago clubs, they occasionally frequented. The only difference was this was Caribbean music, Hip-hop and rap could be detected here and there, adding that little extra something for everyone. At times, the music was almost as spicy and raw as it was in the clubs in Chicago.

Sunshine and White Chocolate leisurely walked the beach looking for a bar that suited their fancy, a comfortable place with good music. It did not take long for them to find Calico Jack's Bar & Grill, just what they were looking for. They gave it a once-over and entered the establishment; they took a table near the band, which was warming up; they were ready to spend an enjoyable evening together.

A waiter came over to greet them. He was dressed in typical Caribbean-style clothing and had a head full of dreadlocks, which looked perfectly natural on him. He looked characteristically Caribbean; there was no mistaking him for anything else. He was tall, dark, handsome, very friendly, and with exceptionally pleasant manners. He introduced himself as Shanka and said, "I'll be your server for the evening. Anything you need, don't hesitate to ask. I'm at your service."

Sunshine asked Shanka, "What's the specialty drink of the house?"

"Mojitos are our specialty, what we're best known for, sir."

"What are the ingredients?" Sunshine asked.

"Our mojitos are made with the finest bay breeze mint sprigs, piña colada, two spoonsful of sweetener, one-part Malibu rum, and just a touch of Galliano liqueur to give it an international flair and blended making up the Caribbean mixture."

Sunshine and White Chocolate looked at each other and smiled. "Two mojitos," he said.

"No problem, mon. Here's some menus. I'll get your drinks."

The music was flowing in earnest by the time Shanka returned with their drinks and took their dinner order. Sunshine had decided on the evening special, a seafood platter that included a dozen large boiled shrimp, a medium Caribbean lobster, a blackened red snapper steak, and a large tossed salad with their special house dressing. White Chocolate ordered a large bowl of clam chowder, a half dozen butterflied fried shrimp, and a small Caesar salad.

Sunshine and White Chocolate enjoyed their mojitos and slowly became mesmerized by the band's intoxicating music. They felt the urge to dance, as several other patrons were already doing. Reaching the small dance floor, they tried to emulate some of the local dance steps but quickly gave up on that and did their own thing.

As they were returning to their table, Shanka arrived with a large tray above his head. As he set the food down, Sunshine told him how much the two of them were enjoying the band.

"The band is local and plays here seven nights a week," Shanka said. "They are one of the more popular bands around. They play from eight o'clock to somewhere around three. I'll tell them how much you enjoy their music. I'm sure they'll appreciate the compliment."

After dinner, Sunshine and White Chocolate danced and danced until midnight. It had been a long day, and the two wanted to sleep before their trip to the farm.

Sunshine caught Shanka's attention and asked, "Could you bring our bill before we leave and forget about paying?"

Shanka chuckled. "I'll total your check and be back shortly."

When he came with the bill, Shanka said, "I've enjoyed being your server. You must promise to come back soon."

Sunshine looked over the bill and pulled out a wad of money. He gave Shanka a well-deserved tip for his outstanding service. "Shanka, we've appreciated your hospitality. If we have time before leaving, we'll drop by and see you again."

"Great," Shanka said, "but if you can't, I'd like to wish you a safe journey back to the states and hope you visit the island again soon."

Sunshine and White Chocolate walked on the beach to their hotel. It had been a long day, and it was time for them to retire.

CHAPTER 7

The following morning, the phone rang. Sunshine rolled over and picked up the phone. "Hello?"

"Good morning, Mr. Lewis. This is the front desk giving you your courtesy wake-up call you asked for when you came in late last evening."

"Yes, thank you," Sunshine said.

White Chocolate asked, "Who was that that called?"

"The front desk. Our wake-up call I asked for when we came back last night."

"Glad we had them call or we would have overslept."

They stayed in bed for a while reminiscing about the previous day and how much they had enjoyed it, but then they got up, showered, and dressed, and they made a quick trip to the dining room for breakfast.

After breakfast, they went outside the hotel to where the tour bus had parked and was picking up other guests going on the trip. They introduced themselves to a young couple sitting across the aisle. After a brief conversation, they learned they were from New York. The couple told White Chocolate they had just gotten married and on their honeymoon.

The driver welcomed everyone aboard and told them to sit back and enjoy the scenery; he said the trip to the farm would take between twenty to thirty minutes. "Of course," he said, "it all depends on traffic." He chuckled like it was a freeway, busy with commuters on their way to work. "On the way, I'm going to give you a heads-up as to what to expect once we arrive."

Along the way, the driver pointed out points of interest as they slowly made their way through the morning rush hour; before long, they were out of town and heading to the farm.

When they arrived, the mini bus stopped in a parking area, where Miguel, their guide, met the group. He welcomed them to the farm and gave them a synopsis of the day's activities. He asked, "How many of you have ridden a horse before?" Only one in the group raised a hand. "Then I guess I'll have to give the rest of you a crash course in how to mount and dismount. It's not rocket science, but it's necessary." Miguel chuckled to himself at the gringos' unfamiliarity with riding. They were no different from the hundreds of other city dwellers he thought of who'd taken the same outing in the past.

After Miguel's short spiel on the correct and incorrect way to mount and dismount a horse, he said, "Folks, it's time to mount up and get this show underway."

One by one, they mounted their horses. Some needed a little help while others didn't, but they were all eager to tour the farm and the newly discovered cave on the back forty. This was a new experience not only for Sunshine and White Chocolate but also for the honeymooning couple. The four of them were a bit apprehensive as they sat in their saddles watching Miguel, who announced, "Let's move out. Follow my lead and do not—I stress do not—stray from the group or trail."

It was not long before everyone gained confidence in their ability to ride; it was not as bad as most had anticipated. Before long, they were riding through the tranquil but barren landscape filled with only large boulders and centuries of lava rock everywhere. Occasionally, someone would spot an animal scurrying through the rocks or a bird taking flight as they disturbed some of the wildlife.

Somewhere along the way, Leroy, the husband of the honeymooning couple, rode up alongside Miguel and asked, "Would it be possible for me to leave the group long enough to relieve myself?"

Leroy had been eyeing a large tree for some time. It was far enough off the trail that he could use that ruse to cover up his purpose in leaving the group. The area was off to the left of the trail and a large boulder near the tree that would give him some privacy.

Miguel told Leroy, "It's normally not permitted, but in your case, I'll make an exception," Miguel said. "Catch up as soon as you can so we all reach the cave at the same time."

"Don't worry," Leroy said. "I'll not be gone long."

Leroy cut his mount from the group and headed to the tree and boulder. After reaching the tree, Leroy dismounted and tethered the reins to a branch before ducking behind the lone tree, where the others couldn't see him. He relieved himself and looked around. He spotted a large indentation under the boulder that was large enough for the backpack he was wearing. It held stolen money with which he was to have paid for drugs he received from a Colombian drug cartel while in Colombia. He and his wife had double-crossed the cartel; they had taken the drugs and kept the money. He and his wife wanted to sell the drugs and use the ill-gotten money to live the good life in the Caribbean.

He stuffed the backpack in the indentation as far back as possible and out of view. It was safe from view and the weather. He returned to his horse, rode back to the trail, and met up with the group. He rode up alongside his wife and gave her a wink.

When they reached the cave, Miguel said, "Time to dismount. If you need my help, let me know."

Some of the older riders shouted out or raised their hands, and Miguel dismounted and helped them down from their saddles. A few in the group congratulated themselves on having ridden to the cave. Though they were a bit sore from sitting in the saddle and a little unsteady on their feet, they considered it an enormously gratifying accomplishment.

Miguel said, "I need you to form a single-file line. It's time to head into the cave and have a look around."

"Why single file?" someone asked.

"The cave entrance is wide enough for only one person at a time."

Leroy thought that if he had not stashed his backpack in the rock, he would not have been able to enter the cave and would have had to leave it outside. It could have been stolen, and all his work and planning would have been for naught.

The group lined up, and Miguel led them to the cave entrance. They realized why the single file was necessary. They started through the narrow entrance, which was almost too narrow for some, but they all made it inside. The cave opened up into a large room; they spread out.

Miguel explained to the group as they plodded along the uneven, damp, slippery rock floor they would see artifacts left behind centuries earlier by the indigenous people who once inhabited the area. When they saw the artifacts, they didn't consider them all that spectacular, but they were interesting nonetheless. The few small statues and antiquities revealed how religious and creative the indigenous people had been. After the short tour, the group left single file once again as they exited the cave.

Miguel asked, "Did you enjoy the cave? What did you think about the artifacts?"

Someone said, "The cave was interesting, and the artifacts were thought-provoking and interesting," but he didn't elaborate more on the subject.

Miguel offered the group a little more history as he led them back on a different trail as they wandered through more lava rocks and sparse vegetation. The farm was basically a barren wasteland compared to farms Sunshine and White Chocolate had seen while driving outside Chicago.

They got back to the barn and dismounted. They waited for the driver to finish conversing with the owner of the farm. He shook hands with the owner and walked back over to the group and asked, "Did you enjoy your trip?" An older couple told him they had, but the others said nothing or just shook their heads.

They rode back to the hotel and said their goodbyes. Some headed to the beach while others went for a late lunch or a cold drink. Sunshine and Leroy made arrangements to meet for dinner at Morgan's Seafood Restaurant that evening. Sunshine and White Chocolate went to their suite to take a late nap and rest before another busy evening.

That evening, as White Chocolate and Sunshine arrived at the restaurant, looked around but did not see Leroy and Shirley. Sunshine asked their waiter, "Have the Smiths called to say they were running late or to cancel their reservation? We were to meet them for dinner."

"As far as I know, no one has canceled reservations this evening, but to be sure, let me check with at the reservation desk."

After a short time, the waiter returned and informed Sunshine that there had been no call or cancellation from anyone by the name of Smith. "I will inform you immediately if they call," he said.

Sunshine and White Chocolate ordered cocktails while awaiting the arrival of the honeymooners. After thirty minutes or so, they decided the Smiths were not coming, and they ordered dinner. After dinner, they enjoyed the music and an after-dinner drink but were then ready to call it a night.

The following morning, they heard on the local TV news that their newfound friends, Leroy and Shirley Smith, had been arrested for smuggling cocaine into the country. Sunshine and White Chocolate were surprised at the turn of events. The news anchor said that the police had been keeping the Smiths under tight surveillance after arriving on the island; it was not their first visit to the island. They had been on the local police's and DEA agents' radar. This was not the first contact with the Smiths as they passed through the Caymans on their way to the states from Colombia.

Prior to their return from the farm the previous day, the police led by Captain Eubanks had searched the Smiths' room at the hotel and had found several pounds of cocaine hidden in the lining of a piece of duffle bag. The authorities assumed that the drugs had been smuggled out of Colombia into the Caymans by the Smiths as they made their way north to the United States.

Unbeknown to them, Sunshine and White Chocolate they found themselves under the police's microscope having been seen associating with them the previous day. They were shocked to learn the supposedly honeymooning couple were mules for a Colombian drug distributor. Sunshine and White Chocolate became paranoid and fearful because of their brief and innocent association with the couple.

It wasn't long until Sunshine heard someone pounding on his door. He yelled, "Hold your horses. I'm dressing and will be there momentarily."

Sunshine finished dressing and opened the door. He was surprised to see three of the biggest policemen he had ever run across.

Captain Eubanks introduced himself and his two senior officers.

Sunshine asked Captain Eubanks, "Yes? What do you want?"

"Would you or your wife have any objections to our searching your suite?" Captain Eubanks asked. "We would like to look around with your permission of course. We have reasonable suspicion there are drugs inside."

"Drugs! Why? Why would you think we have drugs in our possession?"

"We've arrested a couple last evening who claim to be newlyweds here on their honeymoon. I think you know them, Leroy and Shirley Smith. You were seen socializing with them yesterday and were to have dinner with them last night at Morgan's Seafood Restaurant as I understand. Am I correct?"

"Yes, but we met them only yesterday on a farm tour."

"How long have you and your wife known them? Are you and your wife working for the same Colombian cartel? Tell us about your association with the newlyweds."

"We met them for the first time yesterday as I told you on a tour bus going out to the farm. And no, my wife and I don't work for a drug cartel out of Colombia. We were never friends with them."

"We'll check that out, but I had to ask." You understand?

"Yes, I'm sure it looks suspicious, but believe me, it's not as it appears."

"Yesterday, we paid a visit to their room while they were out and found several pounds of cocaine hidden in their duffle bag. We've had an eye on them for some time, and seeing you and your wife with them yesterday piqued our interest. We may need to ask you some questions later on downtown. But if you don't mind, we would like to check your unit while we are here just as a precaution. Would either of you have any objections if we searched the room and your duffle bag?"

"No, but why would you suspect me and my wife of being involved in drug trafficking since we met this couple only yesterday? We had very few things in common. The biggest one was being from the states, but as far as anything else, there was nothing."

"I understand, but we need to look around your suite and personal items just the same."

"Do you have a search warrant?"

"No, but as a matter of courtesy, I asked if you had a problem with our searching your room, didn't I? At which time you said no. Here in the Caymans, a search warrant is not necessary as long as we have reasonable suspicion and or your permission. Your associating with the Smiths gives us probable cause. Now that we understand each other, my men and I will check out your unit. We will let you know when we finish. If you would be so kind as to have your wife join you on the couch until we've completed our search, it would be greatly appreciated."

The search lasted the better part of two hours. Captain Eubanks and his two officers inspected every piece of duffle bag in the closet, checked every piece of clothing, looked under the bed, between the mattresses, and under the chair and couch cushions. They removed the duct covers to look inside, checked the medicine cabinet, opened each bottle, and checked its contents. After finishing an in-depth search of their personal belongs and the unit, Captain Eubanks said, "We have inspected the room for drugs and found nothing. I would like you two to accompany us to police headquarters. I have several questions about what brought you to the Caymans."

White Chocolate and Sunshine followed Captain Eubanks and his policemen out of the hotel and into a police car in front of the hotel. A second police cruiser served as backup on the trip to the station. Sunshine felt like they were being abducted by a mafia hit squad as opposed to the police. No one talked. No one made eye contact. Captain Eubanks was all business.

At police headquarters, Sunshine and White Chocolate were led to separate interrogation rooms. It was quite a while before anyone came back into the room where Sunshine waited. The two policemen Sunshine had met earlier entered the room with a DEA agent and again introduced themselves. They told Sunshine, "We're here to ask you some questions, and if you cooperate, you and your wife will be released and be free to continue your vacation without further interference. So, if you don't mind, let's get started."

"White Chocolate and I have nothing to hide. I'd appreciate it if you would get started. I'm ready to get this over with and get out of here."

"Okay, let's start with when you first met the Smiths."

Their questions continued one after another. Sunshine answered each as honestly and as truthfully as possible. The officers seemed to be in no hurry; they sat silently listing to his answers without interruption. The questions asked by the two officers were methodical, disciplined, and systematic. They did not miss a thing. After a couple of hours of interrogating Sunshine and being satisfied with his answers, the interrogation ended as abruptly as it had begun.

The police officers and the DEA agent looked at each other as if to agree that Sunshine had answered their questions truthfully. Leaving the interrogation room, they acknowledged his story of flying down to the Caymans on business had absolutely no connections with the Smiths before arriving. Sunshine was told he and White Chocolate were free to return to their hotel but not to leave the country until this matter had been fully addressed and settled.

Back in their hotel room, still confused and unsure what to expect next, Sunshine and White Chocolate were at a loss for words. They ordered room service, which was much faster and less trouble than getting cleaned up again and going out.

As they busied themselves rearranging their clothes, duffle bag, and medicines after the visit by police, they heard a knock on the door. They froze. A chill went up their spines. Still in shock at what had occurred earlier, they were paranoid at the sudden knock on the door. After what seemed an eternity, they heard a second knock and someone say in a rather soft voice, "Room service."

At hearing such a melodic voice, the two breathed sighs of relief and laughed.

"The doors open," Sunshine said.

The server entered the room with the cart and saw White Chocolate peeking out the bedroom door. "Where would you like me to put your food, madam?"

"Leave it on the coffee table," White Chocolate said.

After placing several covered dishes and a pot of coffee on the coffee table, he asked Sunshine, "Will there be anything else, sir?"

White Chocolate stuck her head out of the bedroom door. "Thank you. That'll be all for now."

Sunshine tipped the man a five spot and thanked him. The server returned the thanks and quietly exited the room.

Coming out of the bedroom wearing a white house robe and a towel around her hair, White Chocolate uncovered the dishes and sat down next to Sunshine. They were hungry and irritated but immediately began devouring the food. They ate everything on their plates including the dessert.

After satisfying their hunger, it was siesta time. They headed to the bedroom; it had been a long and disturbing day for Sunshine and White Chocolate, a day neither would soon forget. How had they been so lucky to have picked this couple to associate with among the many tourists that day going out to the farm. Lucky them.

CHAPTER 8

Sunshine and White Chocolate had been advised not to leave the Caymans until the matter of the drugs had been cleared-up. They needed to cancel their flight, which had been scheduled the next day. Not knowing when they would be allowed to leave, they had to put their return flight on hold.

White Chocolate called the airlines and explained that they were unsure of when they would be returning to the states. The agent said, "When you learned what day you will be leaving, call back and I'll be happy to assist you in rescheduling your flight." White Chocolate left it at that.

They decided to go out to dinner after such a taxing and unnerving day. They wanted to put the whole episode behind them and return as soon as possible to Chicago, where they could continue their lives as before with no more invasions of their privacy by police or DEA agents.

The following morning, they were rudely awakened by loud knocking. Sunshine crawled out of bed and walked over to find out what all the ruckus was about. He opened the door and saw Captain Eubanks, along with two policemen and DEA agent.

Captain Eubanks said in a rather raspy voice, "Good morning, Mr. Lewis, I hate to bother you so early, but you and your wife will need to accompany us to police headquarters. We need to talk to you about some disturbing issues that have come to our attention since our last meeting. If you would be so kind as to get dressed and accompany us downtown, I would greatly appreciate it."

"What's this all about?" Sunshine asked.

"You'll be told when the time is right. Please get dressed. We'll be in the living room."

Sunshine returned to the bedroom and told White Chocolate, "Captain Eubanks wants us to accompany him back to the police station. He told me something new has come up that he needs to question us about. Hope this is the last time we're harassed by this bunch of yo-yos. I'm sick and tired of the way we're being treated."

"What more do they want from us, Sunshine? We've told them everything we knew about the couple yesterday."

"I know we did. Maybe they've uncovered more on us than they had led us to believe yesterday. Let's find out what it's all about. Until they learn all they can about the situation, they'll not stop hounding us. Get dressed so we can get this over with and get out of this godforsaken country. I'm sure it's just a minor detail. Let's do it so we can get off this island the sooner the better."

Sunshine and White Chocolate knew something was not right but didn't know what.

At the police station, they were again led to separate holding rooms. It was getting to be too much for White Chocolate, who was beginning to worry what was going to happen to her and Sunshine. She wondered what kind of trouble they had gotten themselves into by associating with the honeymooners?

Once the interrogations began, Sunshine and White Chocolate learned separately that the police had checked with the Chicago police and had learned about their illegal drug activities there. As the tangled web and background check continued, things started not looking good for White Chocolate and Sunshine in the Caymans.

Sunshine was questioned at length about his stint in prison and his association with the New York distribution syndicate and specifically a certain individual named Slice.

"We've learned that the two we have in custody are also an integral part of the same New York syndicate," the chief interrogator said. "And that you and this Slice are involved with some sort of illegal drug activities around the Chicago area. Is that correct?"

"I know Slice only as a supplier. He was instrumental in helping me with my business by supplying me with drugs. But I wasn't aware the Smiths and Slice had ties. Like I told you before, I didn't know or had ever met the Smiths prior to our arrival in the Caymans."

"I understand. You've said that before, but I want to know, are you and your wife an extension of the illegal drug trafficking trade being carried out by the New York syndicate? And did they send you to the Caymans to pick up drugs from the Smiths and take them back to Chicago?"

"No, as I've told you before, we came to the Caymans on our own to conduct business with a bank here."

The DEA agent said, "Any way you look at it, Mr. Lewis, it doesn't look good for you and your wife. You need to come clean and cooperate with us. If you do, I assure you things will be much easier for all involved including you and your wife."

Sunshine turned to Chief Eubanks who sat quietly in the corner as the investigation continued. "Like I told you yesterday, we had no idea who those two were when we met them. It was a coincidence meeting the Smiths on the tour bus. They were someone to talk to and enjoy each other's company while vacationing here in the Caymans."

"We've learned from other sources that you and your wife recently made a substantial deposit in one of our local international banking facilities," the chief said. "Can you enlighten us about that and how you happened to come across such a large amount of cash?"

"That's a personal matter. There's no reason for you to know my personal business. It was a private transaction between the bank and me. That's all the information I'm willing to give you."

"I understand your concern and respect your privacy, but you must understand, to us, it looks rather suspicious, would you not agree? Running around the country with such a large amount of cash? And you and your wife suddenly running around in the company of the Smiths from New York, who just happened to be in the possession of several pounds of cocaine? And both of you working alongside the same group out of New York? Coincidence? You tell me."

"It may look suspicious to you, but I'm telling you that you have it all wrong. It's not how it appears. My wife and I didn't come here to purchase illegal drugs. I have my own business back in Chicago. I don't need to hustle drugs in the Caymans. We got involved with the wrong people yesterday and find ourselves under suspicion for something we're not guilty of only because of similar ties to the same organization in New York. That doesn't seem like enough evidence for us to be falsely accused of trafficking in the Caymans."

"Maybe not in your view, but you must admit it does look bad for the lot of you, wouldn't you say?"

"Maybe in your way of thinking but not in mine. We were completely in the dark about what the Smiths were involved in. Just an honest mistake on our part if you can believe that."

"I see your point, Mr. Lewis, but I'm still having a hard time accepting what you say as the truth. I'm sure you see my point. Too many coincidences to suit me. We're going to be making more inquiries into this web of deception, so once again, I'm asking you not to leave the island until we sort out what's really going on here."

"My wife and I need to get back to Chicago and to our business as soon as possible. Is there any way you can expedite the process? My wife as you know by now is pregnant and has an appointment with her gynecologist early next week. It's imperative that she see the doctor since she's recently been diagnosed with high blood pressure. Pregnancy-induced hypertension, which is a major concern for her and her doctor at the moment. If she's not treated properly, she could end up losing the baby. I'm sure you can understand our concern."

"We'll do what we can to ensure quick justice in this matter. It shouldn't take much longer. Let us do a bit more investigating and follow up on several unanswered questions pending in this unusual situation. As you know, this is a sticky business not only in the Caymans but also in the states. I'm sure you are aware of the consequences if we don't get it right."

"Yes, who more than I about consequences of such an undertaking? Been there, done that."

"We're well aware of your colorful past, Mr. Lewis. Thank you and your wife for your understanding and patience. We should be able to wrap this up by the weekend. I promise you that if we find you and your wife weren't involved, you'll be free and on your way. It all depends on the Smiths and their take on the relationship between the two of you."

"Am I free to go?"

"Yes, but don't try leaving the island until we tell you it's okay, okay? Have a nice day, Mr. Lewis, and enjoy our beautiful island."

Sunshine embraced White Chocolate in the lobby of the police headquarters. They headed out for an early lunch since they had missed breakfast again. They found a restaurant in the Westin Grand along the beach and enjoyed a well-deserved lunch as they talked about their situation. They spent the afternoon away from the hustle and bustle of the masses along the beach and enjoyed the moment. They agreed that this was a trip they would never forget. A trip to hell (an area that actually exists on the island)—so fitting.

When they got back to the hotel, they saw Captain Eubanks and his crew including the DEA agent in the lobby. As they approached them, Sunshine could tell something was not right. Captain Eubanks and the others stood as Sunshine neared them.

The DEA agent said, "Bad news, Mr. and Mrs. Lewis. You're under arrest. If you don't mind, I need the two of you to turn around and place your hands at the small of your backs." As he cuffed them, he said, "You have the right to remain silent. Anything you say may be used against you in a court of law. You have the right to consult an attorney before speaking to the police and to have an attorney present during questioning. If the police deny you that request, your rights may have been violated."

This came as a complete surprise to Sunshine and White Chocolate. They wondered what new evidence had been uncovered or learned that warranted their arrest. *Have the Smiths somehow involved us in their drug-running scheme?* Sunshine wondered. *Have they been given some kind of deal to involve us in their smuggling business? So many questions without answers.*

CHAPTER 9

Once again, they were placed in separate interrogation rooms and eventually told of the new evidence provided by Leroy Smith, (which had been previously taped by police and wanted Sunshine to hear.) "I was informed by the New York organization and specifically Slice that when we reached the Caymans, we were to look up a couple from the states by the name of Lewis who were on holiday. And once I found them, I was to tell Sunshine that Slice had informed me that they were to take possession of the cocaine I had and bring it back to the states. The reason the transfer had not been completed was that I was arrested before making arrangements for the exchange. We were to have dinner with the Lewies's two nights ago, at which time I was to inform Mr. Lewis of the exchange. I was to clarify to Mr. Lewis my situation had changed and Slice would be notifying him of the exchange before he and his wife left the island."

After hearing that from Captain Eubanks, Sunshine rolled his eyes. "I can't believe what I've just heard. This doesn't make sense. I can be arrested for something that was going to happen in the future and totally unaware of? Are you serious about pressing charges on such trumped-up innuendos and hearsay?"

"We take the charges seriously. You and your wife are now the newest residents of the Caymans until we can get you before the magistrate and have him hear your case. In the meantime, we'll find a physician to attend to your wife's condition. If we find out anything new surrounding this case, we'll update you."

Captain Eubanks put some folders on the table into his briefcase and left the room along with the DEA agent. Not long after that, a couple of policemen arrived, handcuffed Sunshine, and took him to a holding cell in the smelly, disgusting bowels of the jail that was already overcrowded with five other inmates, four more than the cell had been built to house. It did not take Sunshine long to figure out the pecking order. As low man on the totem pole, he was obligated to take the only empty space on the floor, which was between the toilet and washbasin, the worst location in the cell.

After an hour or so of getting acclimated to his new living facility, he heard a commotion in the hallway. Sunshine saw two large guards dragging a prisoner down the dirty, narrow passageway. After a closer look, he recognized the prisoner as none other than Leroy Smith, who was kicking and screaming with hands cuffed behind his back and restraints around his ankles attached to a clanking chain around his waist. He looked pathetic. Defenseless. Defeated. Despondent.

Sunshine realized that his and White Chocolate's incarceration was more serious than either had imagined when arrested. Still in shock at the harsh conditions, he wondered what choices they had to overcome this latest adversity.

Something suddenly dawned on him. *What's happened to White Chocolate?* He had not seen or spoken to her since leaving the hotel. She and he had traveled in separate cars to the police headquarters. He wondered where she was and how she was holding up. *Is she in an overcrowded cell same as me? Have they been interrogating her? Was she in an infirmary being looked after? What's her status?* He had no way of finding out. The conditions of and attitudes toward prisoners in the Caymans, which reminded Sunshine of a Third World country, was different from that in the states; it was more animalistic. It was survival of the fittest, not the way he envisioned spending the rest of his life after having left the Windy City only a few days earlier.

The cell door opened early the following morning. Sunshine was thoroughly exhausted, hungry, dirty, and sweaty. He was lying on the floor in between the filthy toilet and dirty sink. Two guards yelled his and two others' names. The three were chained and escorted down the dirty, smelly, dark hallway to a holding cell and locked up. They were told that they would stay there until it was time to face the magistrate, learn the charges against them, and have a trial date set. Justice was to be swift and sentencing even swifter. Sunshine was worried that he and White Chocolate may be found guilty of this conveniently unsubstantiated and trumped-up charges.

He was brought into the courtroom and standing alongside several other prisoners before the magistrate. Sunshine waited patiently as each prisoner was read the charges against him and found out if he could bond out or held without bond. Sunshine's time arrived; he stood before the magistrate, who looked over his notes and the charges then down at Sunshine.

"You were in the wrong place at the wrong time and accused of being part of a drug ring working out of Colombia and New York. The court finds you not guilty of all the charges against you. But it is the court's duty to fine you five hundred dollars for court costs and housing."

Sunshine almost collapsed from relief. Two guards led him to a holding room just outside the courtroom, where he was to wait to be released. He peered through a small glass and wire window in the door and saw White Chocolate with her back to him signing papers at a counter. A short time later, two guards came into the holding area and escorted him to another room and removed his chains and handcuffs. On the bench was a paper bag containing his clothes and personal items. "Change into your civilian clothes and let us know when you're finished," one of the guards said.

Sunshine quickly changed clothes and rapped on the door. A guard escorted him to a counter, where he was handed several papers to sign along with a promissory note to pay his fine.

Captain Eubanks came up and told him, "You're lucky. If you and your wife had been found guilty, she would have been given a lesser sentence being an accomplice, but they would have thrown the book at you. Hope this is an eye-opener. I wish you a good life. Keep your nose clean if you know what's good for you." As Captain Eubanks chuckled to himself.

Sunshine and White Chocolate embraced outside the building and headed back to the hotel. Sunshine said, "Once I'm off this godforsaken island, I'll never step foot on it again."

"Never say never. It could come back to haunt you," she replied.

White Chocolate called Cayman Airlines and asked to be rescheduled on the next flight to Chicago; she was told that that would be at seven the next morning. She and Sunshine spent the evening packing for their return trip to Chicago.

The following morning, they arrived at the airport in plenty of time for the flight. They were ready to leave and get as far away from this lunacy as quickly as possible. The got up from their seats as soon as their flight was announced. They wanted to make sure they were among the first in line at the departing gate.

Someone tapped White Chocolate on the shoulder as she stood in line near the departing gate. She turned and saw the infamous Captain Eubanks smiling broadly. Sunshine and White Chocolate had the same thought: *Déjà vu all over again! No! This can't be happening again!* as they turned and looked at each other.

Captain Eubanks looked at Sunshine and then at White Chocolate. "I wanted to personally come this morning and wish you a safe trip and to say I'm sorry for the inconvenience you had to endure this last week. Without your help, we would never have known who this couple was working for in the states or in Colombia. It was a wake-up call for not only you but also for the police and the DEA working here.

"Due to your unintentional involvement in the case, we now know more about the drug trade passing through the Caymans than we've ever know. It'll make following suspected mules and others passing through our small country easier, thanks to you two. Keep your noses clean when you get home. I know it's a difficult business you're in, but give some serious thought to changing occupations."

With that bit of wisdom, Captain Eubanks walked away as they stood in shock looking at each other.

CHAPTER 10

Arriving at O'Hare, they rushed through customs and downstairs to retrieve their duffle bag and to their car in the parking garage. Sunshine through their bags in the trunk as White Chocolate got in the front passenger seat of the car. When Sunshine got in, she said, "It's great to be back in the Good old U. S. of A. Didn't know how much one could miss what one always took for granted." They both chuckled as reality set in.

"I agree," Sunshine said, "but let's not dwell on last week's debacle. Let's concentrate on the future. It's time to get back to business. I'm sure we have a lot to do after having been gone for so long."

Returning home, White Chocolate retrieved the mail from the mailbox as Sunshine brought the duffle bag in. She threw the mail on the coffee table and sat down on the sofa. Sunshine plopped down next to her. They decided to go through the mail later; it just felt good to be back in familiar surroundings and needed to relax. Sunshine kicked off his shoes, put an arm around her, and kissed her cheek.

They sit on the couch for some time reminiscing about their exhausting and almost tragic vacation trip. Sunshine, reached over and picked up a couple of letters Chocolate had set aside from the junk mail which included an odd-looking letter addressed to him. It was postmarked New York, but there was no return address. Sunshine thought that was strange. He opened it. It was from Slice, who had learned of the bust in the Caymans and wanted to know how it had gone down since he was no longer able to contact Leroy or Shirley Smith. Slice ended the letter with, "Contact me as soon as possible after you get this letter." Sunshine wondered what was going on that warranted a letter rather than a call.

He called Slice. "We've just gotten back from the Caymans and found your letter."

"I want to know what the hell happened in the Caymans with you and the Smiths. I've learned from another contact on the island that they've been arrested. I also found out that you and your wife after returning from some trip with them were also detained. I'd asked the Smiths to meet you and hand over the drugs they were in possession of. Apparently, the police and the DEA had them under surveillance. Our CI there told me they'd been under surveillance from the time they left Colombia to the time they arrived in the Caymans. I was informed by the same contact that you were there with your wife, so I figured I could take the heat off the Smiths if they gave you their stash and you brought it back under the radar, but my best-laid plans went awry."

"White Chocolate and I spent several days being interrogated and one night in jail because of your so-called arrangements. I don't appreciate what you did. Don't ever do anything like that again, capiche, bro?"

"Don't get your feathers ruffled, a—hole. This is part of doing business. Take what happened and live with it or get the hell out of the business! I don't need you to tell me what I can and can't do. If you think you can do better without my help, go for it. Otherwise, keep your thoughts to yourself, you capiche a—hole?"

"Guess it's time we part company and I find a new supplier I can rely on and not be used as a whipping boy. I don't appreciate what you did and no longer want to be associated with the likes of you. I'll go it alone going forward."

"Think you're making a big mistake, but you gotta do what you gotta do. Just don't coming running back to me when things turn south."

Slice hung up. Sunshine told White Chocolate, "No longer will I buy drugs from New York. I've lost my distributorship. I gotta find another distributor."

"Won't be the first time," White Chocolate said.

"I'm sure we'll find someone local who's willing to supply us with drugs for the short term. It may take some time to regain trust among local dealers since we've been buying from out of state this last year."

"Money talks and bullshit walks. If we go about this right, we can turn this negative into a positive and be back in business in no time."

It was a culture shock for Sunshine and White Chocolate having to start over basically from scratch. Finding a new distributor locally would be hit or miss for a while, but that was their only avenue to getting back in the game.

Sunshine was up early the next day. He had a lot on his mind. He had to explain to his crew what had happened in the Caymans and that he had lost his distribution privileges with the organization in New York. And needed their help in finding a new supplier locally. He wanted to tell them what needed to be done in the interim while trying to keeping what business still remaining afloat.

Upon his return to the stash house, Sunshine found it in turmoil. Nothing was as it should have been. Even the most trusted of the group were in total disfunction. He told Marcus, his most loyal assistant, to tell the others there would be a meeting in ten minutes in the living room. He needed to get to the bottom of this state of confusion and disorder. He saw only a bunch of yahoos, young men all over the place playing grab-ass with no leadership.

Marcus assembled everyone in the living room and went to Sunshine's office. "Everyone who's shown up for work is in the living room."

Sunshine went to the living room. He looked over the motley group and disheartened at what he saw. They were not the same group he remembered prior to leaving for the Caymans. They looked disheveled and unprofessional. They had reverted to their old habits—drinking, using drugs, and playing grab-ass; just another bunch of young, ragtag individuals who had lost their way. Everything he had done to instill good work ethics had gone out the window. He had to begin again with Marcus's help and whip them back into shape immediately.

After giving a scathing speech to those assembled, he warned them that if they wanted to continue working there, they had to change their ways and follow the rules on the bulletin board in the hallway or they would be history.

Sunshine told Marcus to appoint new leaders for the different sectors of the organization, which needed a stronger structure and stricter authority. Marcus promoted several strong leaders to the top ranks while firing two of the worst offenders.

Taking Marcus aside after the meeting, Sunshine told him, "As long as you abide by the same rules as the others, I'll leave you in charge, but if you don't shape this ragtag bunch of yahoos into shape, you'll be the first one out of here. Put a stop to this madness and establish order now. It'll be a tough battle to regain their confidence, but working together, we'll address the problems directly and resolve them swiftly if you're willing to help me."

Sunshine looked over those assembled hoping it was not too late to turn this dire situation around. He could not imagine the turmoil and mayhem going on at the stash house being gone for only a week. *When the cat's away, the mice will play,* he thought. It was a tough enough world out there to begin with, but to come home to this? He had to pick up the dropped ball and run with it.

Nothing in Sunshine's life had been easy. He'd been down this lonesome road before. The only one he could count on was White Chocolate, the pillar on which he leaned. But at the moment, she was not available. He was on his own.

CHAPTER 11

A few days later, Sunshine with the help of Marcus, found a new supplier, and shortly after, business began turning the corner. It wasn't firing on all cylinders, but with a tweak here and a tweak there, things would slowly come together. Marcus, once again took over, and steered the enterprise in the straight and narrow with the help of the crew. Business again organized, orderly, and disciplined.

Sunshine, struggling with excessive responsibilities, delegated more and more responsibilities to Marcus, giving him more time to handle the important aspects of running the organization and not playing schoolmarm. He surprised himself at what could be accomplished if he put effort into it.

He started visiting different hoods and meeting gang affiliates in and around but to no avail. It was a dog-eat-dog business. The more he tried to unite other groups, the more resistance he met. The Italians, Mexicans, Chinese, and Russians were independent and wanted to remain independent; they didn't want to work together under one big umbrella.

Not long after his one-man attempt to unite the different hoods, he began having trouble with a couple of groups he'd talked to about combining forces. It once more became a killing field out there. As the killing and infighting increased, the police declared a curfew for those eighteen and younger. That of course did not go over with the younger crowd; the rebellion and killings grew exponentially.

Tension mounted; skirmishes increased. Unrest between drug leaders reached a crescendo. It spread quickly throughout Chi-Town, which again become a powder keg. No one in the drug business was immune. Crime ran rampant; muggings, robberies, rapes, drive-bys, and mayhem became the norm and not likely to lessen anytime soon.

The city fathers in their infinite wisdom called on the national guard once again to help control the unbridled situation. It took several days before national guard troops and police patrolling the mean streets were able in slowing down the bedlam. Not long after the appearance of the national guard, the violence began to lessen. The mean streets eventually returned to a controllable stillness and orderliness, and police were able in managing the situation without outside help.

With the desecration and destruction of the city at yet another crossroads, Sunshine wondered when things would ever return to any semblance of order. It was time that the factions got their acts together and stopped the violence and disorder.

Except it was different this time. Animosity developed between local citizens, rival gangs, and law enforcement; it was going to take time to sweep this latest outburst under the rug. Those working the streets had a different culture—new principles and values. It would take time for the hostility and hatred to lessen. Too many dead, too many hurt and disfigured in this latest upsurge of rival dominance. The local populace suffered greatly after this latest volley of violence and mayhem; it left the city hanging on a thin string with little or no hope for the future without social and structural changes. It would take the dedication and perseverance of those responsible to maintain law and order to right this latest outbreak.

Sunshine tried desperately to give to the local populace and the poorer neighborhoods whatever he could to win their favor. He found out quickly it was too little too late. They had no respect for him or anyone like him. It would never be the same for the drug pushers or dealers going forward; they had made their bed and now had to sleep in it.

Several months later, White Chocolate was ready to give birth. After several pseudo signs of delivery, she was sure this time was the real deal. She called Sunshine to pick her up and rush her to the hospital.

He dropped everything and hurried home. He drove as fast as the law allowed to the hospital, where she was immediately admitted. She was taken to a room, where they tried making her as comfortable as possible. She was in a lot of pain, and her vitals were monitored throughout the day. Uncomfortable as she was, she had to endure her distress and anguish until the baby's arrival.

Sunshine stayed by her side during the nine hours it took her to give birth to a six-and-a-half-pound daughter. Mother and daughter came through with flying colors.

Sunshine? Well, that's another story.

After the delivery, Sunshine told White Chocolate, "I'm dog-tired and need to go home and rest. If you need me for anything, have the nurse call me." He leaned over and gently kissed her on the cheek.

After Sunshine left, she closed her eyes and drifted off to sleep. She awoke early the next morning after hearing voices in the hallway. She pressed her call button indicating that she needed a nurse. Soon, a nurse came along, and White Chocolate asked, "Can I see my daughter?" The nurse told her she would check.

Not long after the nurse returned with the baby and handed her to White Chocolate, who shed a few tears as she held her baby for the first time. She looked at the tiny newborn and thought how lucky she was. She gently laid the baby on her chest, pulled back the baby's blanket, and checked out her fingers and toes making sure she was whole. Nothing seemed out of place. She was well developed, perfect. As she gazed at her baby, she thought, *she looks like a little queen. I'm going to name her Queenetta.*

White Chocolate's instincts kicked in. She gently rolled her newborn on her side and drew her to her breast so she could suckle. After a while, the nurse returned and told White Chocolate it was time to take the newborn back to the nursery so she could be monitored for the next few hours.

After a few hours of sleep, Sunshine awoke, hurriedly dressed, and headed to the stash house. He got there just as others were getting ready for the day. Everyone congratulated him on the new addition to his family. He felt good that they took the time to acknowledge his daughter and ask about White Chocolate. He was all smiles, a happy papa, and it showed.

He called Marcus into his office, where he briefed him on the day's activities; telling Marcus he was in charge until his return later that afternoon. Once the stash house was up and running, Sunshine hustled back to the hospital. He found White Chocolate glowing and in good spirits.

"I've been thinking we should name our daughter Queenetta," she said.

"I've been racking my brain for a name, but you've come up with the perfect name. It's a fine name. That's what we'll name her. I want to see her in the nursery."

After observing Queenetta in her bassinet and trying to get her attention without success, Sunshine went to the nurses' station and asked, "When will my wife and daughter be released?"

"Once we're sure your wife is physically ready to leave. We'll let you know. But until then, you need to wait in her room or lounge area," the nurse replied.

Sunshine walked back to White Chocolate's room; she was sitting in a chair by the bed. With a big smile on his face, he kissed her cheek. "You and Queenetta should be coming home tomorrow once it's established that you're physically fit and able to get around without help."

White Chocolate glowed more radiantly; she couldn't have been happier with that news.

Just then, the nurse brought Queenetta to the room and asked, "It's time for her feeding. Do you feel up to it?"

"Yes, I do." The baby had taken to feeding like a fish to water; she knew exactly what to do after being placed in her mother's arms. White Chocolate found it easier to nurse Queenetta sitting in the chair. She was pleased at herself knowing how to handle the situation and how easy she performed this feeding thing.

After feeding time was over, the nurse told White Chocolate that she would return the baby to the nursery and that she should try to rest. "If everything goes well the rest of the day," the nurse said, "you and your baby should be able to leave the hospital tomorrow."

"Thank you! I'm looking forward to getting back home and taking care of my daughter."

The following day, Sunshine got a call from the hospital; his wife and daughter should be ready to leave the facility by ten thirty. He thanked the nurse, and again put Marcus in charge until his return.

A nurse came into the room as White Chocolate was having her breakfast and told her she could leave later in the morning. "I've called your husband about your release. He'll be here to take you home around ten thirty."

The nurse checked mother and daughter once more and deemed them physically and mentally healthy enough to leave the hospital.

Shortly after that, a nurse arrived with a wheelchair. White Chocolate handed her infant to the nurse and got in the wheelchair. The nurse handed the baby back to White Chocolate as she wheeled them to the elevator, then through the lobby, and out to the pick-up/drop-off area in front of the hospital.

Sunshine was waiting by the car when White Chocolate and daughter appeared. They were wheeled to his car and helped inside. White Chocolate was strapped in while holding Queenetta for the ride home.

"Sunshine, I'm so happy to be going home with you and our baby. This has been a dream of mine since I met you. This is what I've always dreamed of being, a real family."

"I'm grateful too to have such a wonderful person as you and now a beautiful daughter."

Back home, Sunshine helped White Chocolate holding Queenetta out of the car, up the steps, and onto to the porch. As they were about to enter the house, Sunshine spotted a small package wrapped in a brown paper bag, tied with twine leaning up against the house. He took a closer look and noticed that there was no name or return address, only his name in big, bold letters.

He picked up the package off the porch while following White

Chocolate and Queenetta inside. He placed the package on the coffee table as he helped White Chocolate and Queenetta get settled on the couch. He sat down next to White Chocolate then reached over and picked up the package off the coffee table. He untied the twine holding the wrapped package in both hands while he unwrapped it slowly and then opened it. To his amazement, inside the package was a live coral snake. He replaced the lid quickly and put the box back down on the coffee table. He immediately began tying the box up and then took it outside placing it back on the porch. He had to make sense out of what had just happened.

He went inside and told White Chocolate, who was still holding Queenetta, what was in the box. She was petrified. He took her hand. "You are not to answer the door when I'm not home. Keep the doors locked at all times, and keep a lookout for anything suspicious when you're home alone. Whoever this was that thought up this sick joke is looking for trouble, they've come to the right place. They'll be sorry if and when I find them you can take that to the bank."

White Chocolate asked, "Whom do you know with such a sick sense of humor? Who would think of doing such a pathetic thing?"

"I don't know, but I'm going to find out. When I do, all hell's going to break loose. You have my word."

The following morning, he put the box in his trunk and drove to work. At the stash house, he retrieved the box from the trunk and carefully carried it inside. He told Marcus to gather the troops in the living room. Marcus did so and let Sunshine know they had assembled and awaiting his presence. Sunshine took the box from his small office into the living room where he told those assembled, "I found this box on my porch after returning from the hospital with my wife and baby girl yesterday. A poisonous coral snake was coiled up inside, would any of you know or have any idea who may have done this and why?"

The troops shook their heads in disbelief. Several expressed their amazement that anyone would have sent such a macabre, unorthodox message. Whoever had done that was letting Sunshine know the danger he and his family faced.

Sunshine wanted to get to the bottom of this soon before someone close to him was hurt or killed. "Keep your eyes and ears open. If you hear any talk about this, I want to know immediately, understood?"

"Understood?" They all answered in the affirmative.

He didn't know which avenue to take going forward, but he had to involve others who could help him quell this latest debacle. His first thought was to contact the police, but he decided to hire a private investigator, someone who could snoop around and find out who had done this dastardly deed on the QT. Then, Sunshine would handle the situation without interference from the police. He called Al Mendez, a private eye, and set up a meeting for that afternoon in his office.

Later that afternoon, Sunshine was ordering a drug shipment from a local distributor when Marcus came into his office. "There's an Al Mendez in the living room waiting to see you." He told Marcus that he had been expecting Mendez and to send him to the office.

Mendez walked into the office, shook hands with Sunshine, and was asked to have a seat. After some informal chitchat, Sunshine got to the crux of the matter. He explained to Al the situation and asked, "Would you help me find the culprit behind this?"

"This is a strange one, a first for me, but I think I can help you. It'll take time to get my feelers out, but I'm sure I can find out who did this. I'll get on it immediately," Mendez said.

After Mendez left, Sunshine went back to work hoping he had had made the right decision in hiring the PI.

Having grown up in Chicago and being well versed in its underworld workings, Mendez was unsurpassed in his ability to gather information. Over the years, he had amassed a number of contacts, CIs, to call for information vital to his many investigations. His contacts had information they would give only to him because they trusted him and he trusted them.

At the end of the day, Sunshine was mentally and physically

exhausted, ready to go home, to relax away from the taxing situation he found himself in. And couldn't wait to see White Chocolate and daughter after such a hectic and trying day.

CHAPTER 12

After reflecting back on his choice hiring a PI, Sunshine was sure he had done the right thing hiring Mendez, who seemed interested in helping him find out who had sent him the snake and why. He felt better having a professional looking for those who were threatening his family, rather than the police.

Returning home that evening, Sunshine found White Chocolate bewildered and devastated. He asked, "What's wrong?"

She could not answer because of her mental uncertainty.

"What's wrong? What's happened? Tell me!"

"Someone called and threatened to kill me and my family if you didn't stop doing what you were doing and leave Chicago!"

"What did they say I was doing that caused them to go off on you?"

"I don't know, but whoever it was told me you were running your business in an underhanded way and cutting into their profits. He said that if you didn't cease immediately, bad things would happen. I tried to reason with him, but to no avail. He said it had gone on way too long and you needed to get out of town. What are we going to do now that the baby is here?"

"I don't know, but I'm going back to the stash house and inform the group that a turf war is looming and to get ready. I hired a private investigator this afternoon whom I need to inform about this latest threat. At least now we know it has to do with the local drug lords. I won't stop until this matter is squashed; I promise you."

"We need to get this matter behind us so we can get on with our lives. I can't live like this. Things are beginning to unravel all around us. It has to stop. I'm scared!"

"Be patient. Give me a little more time. I'll be back soon. Don't answer the phone or go outside until I get back. I'll get the word out and see if I can stem the tide until this is settled. Wish I knew who was behind this madness, but until then, I'll have to play it by ear."

He kissed her cheek and left.

As he neared the stash house, he saw a number of police milling around the area. They were there investigating a drive-by shooting. Police vehicles were scattered throughout the neighborhood. They were questioning residents about what they had heard and seen. They were having a hard time putting the pieces together in a cohesive way since there were so many conflicting reports of the event. Some said two cars were involved, while others said only one car was involved. Several witnesses told the police that they had seen more than three people in a car with rifles sticking out the windows shooting randomly at anything that moved. Others said that they had seen two people in the cars shooting with what looked like handguns stuck through the windows. It was difficult for the police to determine how many cars were involved, how many weapons, the color of the cars, their makes and models, the number of people involved, or the types of weapons used let alone the gang that caused the melee.

Sunshine found his troops in disarray and near panic. After learning of another drive-by that had left three wounded and one dead, Sunshine was beside himself. No one knew what was going on or what to do. He realized he had to get his act together and learn who was responsible for this gutless act and put a stop to it. He asked the group, "Anyone have any idea who did the drive-by?"

"We think it was Latinos," a corner boy said. "We talked to a couple of street boys as we passed a corner near where the incident occurred and was told it was Latinos. The corner boys were working the next corner a block away when two cars sped past. The corner boys indicated they recognized the colors worn by those in the cars."

Sunshine felt he had a better handle on the situation and would try quelling the turf war that was once again brewing between the two rival gangs. He called White Chocolate. "We've had another drive-by this afternoon near the stash house. Be cautious and extremely careful whatever you do. I'll be home as soon as possible to take care of you and the baby." He hung up and returned to the pressing issues he faced around the stash house.

Gathering the troops once again in the living room, he told them, "You need to keep cool, calm, and collected until this danger is thwarted. I don't want anyone here doing anything foolish that will endanger the rest of the group, understood?" He gathered his street enforcers after the general meeting and said, "Get ready to hit the streets and take care of the problem."

It did not take long before a carload of the Source's street enforcers led by Marcus were on their way to the Latinos' turf to retaliate. Reaching the outer perimeter or invisible line drawn between the two factions, they parked their car.

They got out with weapons in hand and spread out to shoot as many Latinos in certain color clothing as they could locate. After killing and wounding several members of the Latino gang, the Source quickly returned to their car and drove back to the stash house to give Sunshine an update.

Luckily, only two boys belonging to the street enforcers had been injured during this latest confrontation between the opposing parties. Sunshine learned later that three Latinos had been killed and that several others, severely injured, and rushed to a hospital.

It did not take long for a surprise visit from the police. They turned up at the front door of the stash house just hours after the melee. They arrived in force and immediately surrounded the stash house. The officer in charge walked up on the front porch and knocked.

Sunshine and his group were desperately trying to flush or hide drugs scattered around the house in plain sight but to no avail. Too much to dispose of on such notice. Finally, someone inside the house was told to open the door. The police ask the individual standing at the door, "Is Mr. Lewis around? We want to come in and talk to him."

Sunshine knew they wanted to question him about the latest outburst in the Latino neighborhood. He walked to the front of the house, where the police had gathered, and asked the policeman who appeared to be in charge, "To what do I owe this pleasure?"

"Our sources including some of the Latinos involved in an incident earlier tell us you and or your group may have been involved. We've identified three Latin Kings gang members who were killed and three who were wounded. They told us that they thought it was your group who attacked them. We'll interrogate the rest of the group once they're able to talk to us. We'd like you and your group to come downtown with us. We want to get to the bottom of this latest fiasco and clear it up. It shouldn't take long if you're truthful about your activities earlier. I need all of you to follow me out to the waiting cars. We're taking you to the precinct over on Spencer Street."

Sunshine knew this was not going to turn out well. He turned to the group standing around looking for guidance. Sunshine said, "Do what's right. This shouldn't take long if we stick to our guns and keep our mouths shut. Marcus, we'll finish cleaning up the place. Make sure to lock the doors. Don't want anyone snooping around while we're gone."

Marcus replied, "Don't worry. When we return, I'll take the rest of the trash out to the alley before the garbage truck arrives." He winked at Sunshine.

Sunshine and the others followed the police to the patrol cars for the ride to the station. When they got there, they were taken to several large interview rooms with nothing more than a table, a couple of chairs, and a TV camera in the corner of each room.

The police did not immediately begin questioning the group; they let them sit and contemplate their predicament. About half an hour later, several investigators entered the different rooms with coffee, legal pads, and pencils. Sunshine figured it would be a long day. He calmly asked an investigator, "Can I call my wife?"

"Not until after the interview," the investigator said.

He hoped anyone arriving at the stash house would think to call

White Chocolate and tell her what had happened. *One of the latecomers will think to do that*, he thought.

One by one, they were read their rights and asked for their full names. Sunshine said, "My name is Alfonso Lewis, and I live just off South King, but I don't remember the address since it's my girlfriend's house."

"How long have you lived at that address with your girlfriend?"

"Going on two years or thereabouts."

"Mr. Lewis, what do you do for a living?"

"I'm an entrepreneur."

"What is the nature of your entrepreneurial business?"

"I'd rather not say."

"Where were you earlier, say, around eight thirty this morning?"

"At work trying to make a living."

"Are you sure you weren't in the Latin Kings' neighborhood with some of your group causing problems?"

"Don't know what you're talking about. Why would I be over there? They're my rivals in business, and I respect their territory just as they respect mine."

"That's not what we hear. We heard they assaulted your hood recently and killed a couple of your boys. What happened earlier this morning is I think you retaliated, am I right?"

"No. You have the wrong person. I was at work taking care of business until you arrived."

"Can you back your statement up if push comes to shove?"

"I think so."

"Okay, let's establish a time line. At what time did you leave your house this morning?"

"At seven thirty. I got at work around seven forty-five. I was in my office when the police arrived around ten."

"We have reason to believe you along with several of your group earlier paid a visit to the Latinos' hood. We have several eyewitnesses who claim they saw your group in the area where the melee occurred. We have several sworn statements about your group being present at the scene."

"All I can say is whoever gave you those statements is lying. They're just rumors or misleading information. The Latinos would say anything to get one up on my group. We've always been at odds with them as you know. Unless you can prove beyond a shadow of a doubt that I was there with, let's say, pictures, the information you say you have is hearsay as far as I'm concerned. Even if I was in and around that neighborhood, last time I checked, it was still a free country, and I'm allowed to go where I choose, correct?"

"Not quite that black or white or simple as you make it out to be with that last remark," replied the investigator. "We have sworn statements, and those are admissible in court."

"I've had enough of your accusations and insinuations. I want to see my lawyer."

With that declaration, Sunshine ended the interrogation. The investigators exited the room without another word. Sunshine was left alone waiting for permission to make his call.

Not long later, an officer entered the room and told Sunshine, "Follow me."

Sunshine walked behind him down the hallway to a pay phone and was told, "Make your one call. When you're finished, go to the sitting area over there."

Sunshine called his lawyer and briefly explained that he and his group had been picked up and taken to the precinct for questioning. He told his lawyer, "I need you to come down to the jail after posting our bail so me and my boys can return to work."

Not long later, Samuel Lowenstein, his lawyer, arrived at the precinct after posting bail. Sunshine thanked him. After signing the paperwork, the two left the precinct.

Lowenstein told Sunshine, "Be in my office in the morning at nine o'clock so I can start on the paperwork that needs filled out and filed following your release on bail."

They shook hands and parted ways. Sunshine and his crew, who by that time had amassed outside, were ready to return to the stash house and work.

Sunshine had a lot riding on his lawyer. He had a long and rocky road ahead before this latest set of circumstances would be over if it ever was. He called the stash house from a pay phone and talked to one of the street boys who had arrived after the others had been taken to the police station. Sunshine told him, "I'm in front of the police station on Spencer Street. Have some of the boys drive down and pick up me and the rest of the group."

"I'll send Juju and a couple of boys down. They'll be there soon," the street boy said.

Juju and two others drove to the police station and found Sunshine and the others standing on the corner looking bedraggled. It was not long before they were all back at the stash house.

Sunshine asked Marcus, "You and your crew clean the place out before the police come back. Don't want any more charges against me than I have already, understand?"

"Yes. Me and the boys will take the stash over to that abandoned house we use for storage and hide everything in the attic."

Sunshine later walked around looking in the different rooms and knew the place would pass the smell test if police decided to return for further questioning of him or his misfits. Another visit by the police was a given. They would lie low a few days until this thing had time to settle down; they would push the drug business to the back burner. It was going to be a difficult time for the Source, but they had to lie low for a while until this latest fiasco was behind them.

The courts were full of cases of killing, robbery, extortion, rape, arson, and assault all awaiting trial dates. Thousands of cases were on the back burner and nowhere near being placed on the court docket. The court system in Chicago was so backed up that it would take months if not years for most of them to be heard. Meantime, Sunshine had to be vigilant.

Sunshine and his lawyer figured out some sort of plea deal that would satisfy the prosecution and the defense. With luck, the charges might be dismissed or reduced prior to a hearing.

The charges concerning the Latino incident were not something he was proud of, but considered necessary to repay them for what they did to his group. Maybe the court would go easy on him when and if he appeared and able to tell his side of the story. His life hung in the balance until the prehearing. It would be in the judge's, his lawyer's, and the jury's hands. Life with White Chocolate and his daughter was at this point in time was uncertain. His chances of beating the murder charges were the same as throwing sevens, ten consecutives times in a dice game. His chances of acquittal at that point were slim to none. If convicted of any of the charges against him, it would be his third strike, and that meant life in prison.

CHAPTER 13

After checking the stash house thoroughly, Sunshine told Marcus, "Send the boys home until things settle down. I'll let you know when to notify them to return. Tell them to keep their noses clean, and no loose talk about what occurred. That's compulsory. Do I make myself clear?"

"Yes, I'll get on it right away."

It was a difficult decision letting the boys leave, but it had to be done.

After things at the stash house were taken care of, Sunshine went home, where he found White Chocolate changing Queenetta's diaper. That was totally new and alien to Sunshine, who had never been around babies in his life and knew nothing about such stuff. He watched White Chocolate clean up Queenetta and sprinkle baby powder on her. Sunshine asked many questions every time White Chocolate did something new or different. He wanted to know what she did in case he had to handle the same chore down the road. He seemed interested in the smallest detail, and was a quick learner.

A few days later, Mendez called him and said, "I have a positive ID on the individual who left the package on your porch. It was one of the Latinos killed in a turf war on the West Side recently. His name was Hector Lopez. He was one of the Latin Kings' kingpins. If there's anything else I can help you with, call me. I'll send the information along with my bill to your home address. It's been a pleasure doing business with you, Mr. Lewis."

Sunshine thought about he just heard from Mendez, and realized the search for justice had been swift, a waste of his time and Mendez's time. At least he knew who it was and it had been gang-associated. If anything like that happened again, he knew whom to call.

Right after that, Lowenstein called.

"Sam, what have you decided to do about the charges against me?"

"We need to meet soon and discuss your situation?" That's why I'm calling. I need to see you so I can go over the charges with you; and explain what we're up against and what we need to do. How about we meet tomorrow in my office," say around at ten?"

"I'll be there. Hope you have good news. I could use some good news about now."

"Don't know about good news, but I'll explain everything in detail when I see you."

Sunshine had noted the urgency in Lowenstein's voice. He was having disquieting thoughts about the meeting the next day. He wondered what Lowenstein had found out since they had talked last and if it had anything to do with what Mendez had told him about Hector Lopez. *Why would that have any bearing on the case?* He questioned.

As he was trying to get his head around the calls from Mendez and Lowenstein, he heard a loud noise at the back of the stash house. He went out of his office and down the hallway to investigate. He saw smoke billowing throughout the rear of the house. The kitchen was already engulfed in smoke and flames. The fire was spreading quickly throughout the rear of the house and would soon spread down the hall to the rest of the house.

He ran back to his office and gathering what personal belongings he could, and he yelled to the others inside to get out. Everyone immediately fled the old wooden structure as the fire spread at a phenomenal rate from the back of the house to the front and igniting the upper floor as it traveled forward. They were lucky to have gotten out when they did thanks to Sunshine's quick action and thinking.

Fire trucks from two stations arrived, but by the time they set up their equipment, the fire had become so intense that firefighters were unable in containing it. Smoke and flames soon were billowing out the second-story windows and roof in an outward and undulating motion.

The house was beyond saving. The best firefighters could do was keep the fire from spreading to other houses in the area.

Sunshine watched helplessly as the structure burned to the ground. He did not know what to do. *Who did this? Why?* he asked himself as his stash house went up in flames and smoke.

The police arrived and set up a security perimeter to keep unauthorized persons from getting close and hampering firefighters. It took firefighters time to get the fire under control, but finally, there was light at the end of the tunnel. Once the fire burned itself out, investigators could now enter the property and try to determine the origin or cause of the fire. Since the fire investigators had not talked to Sunshine, and the cause of the fire still unknown. Sunshine would wait to talk to the fire investigators and explain what he heard and witnessed as the fire began in the back of the house and quickly spread through the house. It was arson, caused by some incendiary device like a Molotov Cocktail. A bottle filled with flammable liquid with a means of ignition or setting on fire before throwing.

A police officer approached Sunshine and asked, "Wasn't that your house?"

"Yes."

"Do you have an idea how the fire started?"

"I think it was a fire bomb thrown into the house by someone in the alley."

"When we get through here, I want you to come with me to the station so I can get your statement. Sounds like you believe it was set intentionally. We need to get a handle on it as soon as possible. Get your stuff and together and wait here until I return."

Many neighbors by that time had gathered around the scene, but the crime scene tape kept most of the rubberneckers back and out of the way. Firefighters on ladder trucks were still spraying water on what was left of the house. It was not long as the remains of the house collapsed in a big swoosh of dust, flame, and smoke. The firefighters doused the smoldering embers in the rubble until they were out. Once firefighters were satisfied the fire was under control, began rolling up the hundreds of feet of hoses and collecting their equipment now scattered over most of the front and back yard.

The police officer who talked to Sunshine earlier came back and said, "Get your things together and put them in the back seat of my squad car. I'll take you downtown for your statement."

Sunshine wanted to call White Chocolate, but there was no time. Placing what few items he had gathered before leaving the house in the back seat of the car, he crawled in the front seat with the policeman and whisked away to the police station downtown.

At the station, he was led to an interview room to wait.

Minutes later, Lowenstein showed up. Sunshine asked, "What are you doing here? Who told you I was here?"

"I was visiting another client, and as I was finishing up, I saw you being escorted in. I dropped by the front desk before leaving and told the desk sergeant I was your lawyer and asked if I could speak to you. The sergeant was hesitant, but he told me to hang loose for a minute and he would find out if that was possible without an appointment.

It was and here I am. I wanted to talk with you before leaving. "Why are you here?"

"Earlier while working in my office I heard a loud noise in back of the house. When I left my office to investigate the noise, I looked down the hallway toward the kitchen, and all I saw was smoke and flames. I told the others to leave, and we all got out. By the time we did, the house was engulfed in smoke and flames."

"Do you have any idea who or what caused the fire?"

"Not really. Like I said, it erupted into a fireball so fast that I barely had time to yell at the troops to get out. I have an idea who the responsible party is, but without witnessing the incident, I can't prove it. But I'm sure I'll eventually learn who it was."

"Since there's nothing else to discuss right now, I'm leaving for another appointment. We'll meet tomorrow morning at ten as scheduled. I have a few things we need to discuss and a couple of lingering questions about your case."

"I'll be there if nothing else happens. If something comes up, I'll call. Thanks for dropping by." Lowenstein left.

Sunshine was once again alone in the interrogation room contemplating this newest quandary, he found himself. With so many things stacking up against him, he was finding it more and more difficult to think rationally about what was going on in his life. He wanted to call White Chocolate. He got up and walked out into the hallway and found a public phone hanging on the wall. White Chocolate was surprised to hear his voice since he rarely called from work. After telling her about the fire and where he was, she was shaken and visibly upset.

After she settled down a bit, Sunshine asked, "Are you okay?"

"Yes, but emotionally shaken up."

"I understand. I'm upset too. I need to get to the bottom of this soon and stop this insanity before it compounds and more people get hurt or killed."

"Don't do anything foolish. We have a daughter who needs a father, and I need you too."

"I promise I'm not going to do anything foolish. I've learned my lesson and will travel the straight and narrow. I can't take much more of this, it's becoming too dangerous. I'm getting out of the business as soon as all this mess I've gotten myself into is over. I still have a lot on my plate, and I've put you and Queenetta in danger."

"I'll hold you to that promise," as Sunshine hung up the phone and back to the interrogation room.

Not long after his return to the interrogation room, a couple of detectives arrived with a tape recorder, sharp pencils, notepads, and something to drink. "Would you like something cold to drink before we get started?" they asked.

"Yes. A Coke would be fine."

One of the detectives left to get him the Coke. When he returned, handed him the coke and asked, "Are you ready to proceed?"

"Yes," Sunshine said.

The detectives introduced themselves and asked, "Do you have any objections to being taped?"

"Do I have a choice?"

"Yes and no. It just makes the interview easier to verify in case of a problem or dispute down the road. I'm sure you understand."

"Yes, but I'm not in the best frame of mind at this time, and if I make a misstatement during the taping, will I be able to correct it and start again?"

"We normally don't permit such a thing, but in your case, we'll allow it. You ready?"

"As ready as I'll ever be under the circumstances."

One detective turned on the tape recorder and said, "For the record, let's begin with your full name."

"Alfonso Lewis."

"Mr. Lewis, tell us in your own words what you think led up to the fire this morning at approximately seven forty-five a.m. at your place of business?"

"I arrived at work at my regular time, a little before eight. I was in my office catching up on paperwork when I heard a loud noise, maybe five minutes later, toward the rear of the house. I got up to check on the noise, and as I stuck my head out the door and looked down the hallway toward the kitchen, I saw flames and smoke billowing from under and around the back door."

Sunshine told them about grabbing some things from his office and yelling at the others to get out as the smoke and fire by that time was racing through kitchen and approaching the hallway.

"It happened so fast that I don't remember racing down the steps into the yard and winding up across the street. Next thing I recall was sitting on the ground in my neighbor's yard and watching fire trucks racing up and down the street with lights flashing and that godawful horn blaring. I don't remember anything else until one of your police officers approached me to find out if I was okay."

"Since you don't remember anything else at this time, I'm going to end our session. If we need to talk to you more about the fire, I'll call or drop by your house. Thanks for your help. You're free to go."

Sunshine left the room and as he was leaving picked up the phone in the hallway and called Marcus at home. "Marcus, I need you to drive to the police station downtown and pick me up, then drive me home. I'm being cut loose here."

Marcus arrived at the police station in a matter of minutes; Sunshine saw him pulling into the parking lot, while still inside the police station, opened the door and walked over to the car and got in. As Marcus was exiting the parking lot, Sunshine had second thoughts about going straight home.

"I changed my mind about going straight home. Drive me by the stash house. I want to see what's left of the place."

Reaching the stash house, Marcus drove slowly down the street so Sunshine could see what remained of the burned-out structure. Sunshine saw two groups of Latinos sitting in their cars on a side street half a block down. He assumed they were making sure the house was completely destroyed so they could report to their boss on their total success.

"Drive around the block, Marcus. I want to check out the two cars of Latinos I saw parked on the side street as we drove by."

But by the time they circled the block, the two cars had vanished into thin air. Sunshine guessed that they had seen him and Marcus. But Sunshine had gotten got a good look at the two cars as they drove by the first time. The cars were not your everyday looking cars. Both had special paint—cherry red with sparkles—and impressive stainless-steel rims. One even had a foxtail hanging from its radio antenna—easily recognizable.

Marcus took Sunshine home and dropped him off. Sunshine went in and found White Chocolate on the couch holding Queenetta. He laid the jumbled stack of papers he had grabbed from his office on the stand near the door and gave White Chocolate a kiss on her forehead.

"Were they able to save the stash house?" she asked.

"No, it's gone. A total loss. Guess we'll have to use the old storage house until we find a suitable place. At least the drugs weren't inside. I'd had Marcus and the boys move them to the old storage house when they arrested me and charged me with murder, so all was not lost. If anything happens to me, you'll be able to continue business at the old location."

Sunshine sat beside White Chocolate, and both began doting over Queenetta.

"It shouldn't be long before I'm able to get back to work," she said. "Queenetta is big enough that I can start leaving her with a sitter part of the day while I'm away. I've been looking forward to working again. I've missed the action and camaraderie with the group. Let me know when you're ready for me to return so I can find a sitter. I know it's been difficult on you these past few months without my help. I can't wait to get back into the game. You'll have a lot more on your plate in the coming months being busy with legal matters and all. I'm just glad I'm able to step up to the plate and help out while you deal with your legal matters."

A few days later, Sunshine and his group went to the old storage house to get things back in order. It would be like old times—selling and distributing drugs in the old neighborhood. It would take some time to get things reestablished, but Sunshine figured that as word got out, it would be business as usual in no time. He had had a good reputation prior to leaving the old neighborhood. The only problem was that he had to tread lightly and carry a big stick. Reestablishing his territory in this wild and crazy neighborhood would not be a cakewalk. And reestablishing his business there was just the first step. He wanted his business to flourish again.

White Chocolate's being back on board would be a big plus when it came to rebuilding their ties with the locals. She was Sunshine's Rock of Gibraltar. They looked forward to the day she would return and relieve him of the tremendous strain Sunshine had shouldered during her absence. But things looked a little iffy with the murder charge hanging over his head. It was the main encumbrance facing them. They had to come face to face with reality and accept the unknown until Sunshine was convicted or exonerated. Until then, they would run the business as usual and hope for the best.

CHAPTER 14

Almost a year after they returned from the Caymans and moved back into the old neighborhood, things were moving along smoothly when out of the blue a letter addressed to Sunshine was delivered to him as he sat in his office. It was postmarked the Caymans. The return address was from the prison where Leroy Smith had been sent after Sunshine's and White Chocolate's departure from the island. Sunshine was a bit leery about the letter, but opened it and read it. Shirley, Leroy's wife, had given birth to a daughter while in prison and asking for his and White Chocolate's help. He asked if Sunshine and White Chocolate would fly back down to the Caymans and pick up their daughter from the prison where Shirley was incarcerated.

They were desperate to find someone to take their daughter and give her a good home away from the hellhole she was living in. No family members or friends were willing to take on the responsibility of their young daughter. They were desperate not wanting their daughter taken by the local authorities and placed in some evil foster home with God only knew whom.

Having known Sunshine and White Chocolate for such a short period of time, the Smiths grasping at straws; wanted to give their daughter to someone they knew was able to raise and care for her back in the states instead of anyone in that godforsaken place. Shirley's prison was deplorable.

Sunshine gave the letter to White Chocolate. She read it, as several tiny tears trickled down her cheek. She was taken aback by the Smiths' request.

For the next several days, they talked about the pros and cons of taking on such a huge responsibility—another child. But in the end, decided to accept the challenge. They flew to the Caymans once again this time to pick up the baby. They figured that in the states, the infant would have a fighting chance to grow up in a safe environment. A big decision on their part, but considering the joy Queenetta gave them, this was a no-brainer. They didn't want to think about what could happen if they did nothing.

White Chocolate learned after delivering Queenetta that she was no longer capable of having other children. She and Sunshine wanted more, but White Chocolate would never be able to conceive. This was the answer to their prayers—a sibling for Queenetta to grow up with rather than living the lonely life of an only child.

After getting their affairs in order and permission from the courts, they flew to the Caymans for the adoption process. They went to the prison and met with Shirley and her baby Cedrica. After several meetings and filling out the necessary forms, eventually satisfying all the requirements for adoption. Knew they faced many hurdles back in Chicago, but would save that for another day.

Shirley told them she and Leroy appreciated what they were doing and would always be grateful. As they were saying their goodbyes, Shirley kissed little Cedrica with sadness prior to handing her over to White Chocolate. The guards told her it was time to return to her cell. As she was being led away, she took one last look at her daughter.

White Chocolate and Sunshine walked out of the prison with Cedrica, and took a cab directly to the airport. At the airport, they had problems with customs, which they were able to handled and eventually granted permission to leave with the baby. It had been a trying time for all concerned, but that ended as soon as they boarded the plane for their flight to Chicago.

Arriving in Chicago after a few hours' delay in Miami, White Chocolate and Sunshine found themselves with more responsibility than they ever imagined. With murder charges facing Sunshine and new daughter, his world had turned a hundred and eighty degrees. The normal complications of daily life were going to be tenfold, but White Chocolate being the alpha member of the family, it would flourish.

Arriving home, White Chocolate introduced the two infant girls, and they seemed happy in their new roles. The Lewis family was now complete.

Sunshine met Lowenstein to discuss a letter the attorney received from the prosecutor's office saying it was dropping the first-degree murder charge since they had no eyewitnesses. They had not found solid evidence connecting him to the crime scene and no new evidence in the case had surfaced. Sunshine still faced lesser charges, which would hang over his head for the next several months. Waiting for a court date was worse than facing the minor infractions. It was the unknown he and White Chocolate found it difficult to live with.

A year later, Lowenstein told Sunshine that a court date on the lesser charges had been set for three weeks from then. The fat lady was about to sing.

When Sunshine appeared in court, the judge asked how he pleaded. Sunshine replied, "Not guilty, your honor."

The prosecution had to prove without a showdown of a doubt Sunshine guilt, and the only two potential witnesses were dead and three others Latino gangbangers were not sure who did the killing. Lowenstein figured he had better that a fifty-fifty chance of getting the case thrown out on technicalities. Its case was looking good for Sunshine. Since the Chicago court system was so overwhelmed with cases, it had begun throwing out numbers of criminal and domestic cases on the docket waiting to be heard.

Lowenstein got together with the prosecuting attorneys to negotiate a deal, hoping to get the case dismissed for lack of evidence or tossed on a technicality.

In the end, the charges against Sunshine were dropped because of inconsistencies in the testimony fabricated by known criminals telling untruths, hearsay, and lack of evidence. Sunshine was freed, but the judge warned him, "If you are again brought before the courts one more time and found guilty, you'll be sentenced to the maximum allowed by the law, life in prison."

Sunshine was overjoyed for himself and his family. He was again free, but knew in his heart of hearts that he had to change his lifestyle and walk the straight and narrow. He felt a big burden had been lifted from his shoulders. It had been a long, arduous journey, and he was relieved that it was finally over for his family's sake.

Sunshine asked Lowenstein, "How about lunch before settling up?"

"Good idea. I could use something to eat and drink after such an exasperating morning."

After lunch, Sunshine followed Lowenstein to his office to settle his account, and told Lowenstein, "I certainly appreciate all the time you spent working my case, Sam. I can never repay you properly. My family and I will forever be in your debt."

Leaving Lowenstein's office on that note, Sunshine drove back to the stash house, where he was greeted with much enthusiasm on his acquittal. Especially proud was White Chocolate. Life for the two of them could now return to some kind of normalcy at work and home.

CHAPTER 15

It was not long after being acquitted things once again began to wane in Sunshine's life.

A street boy returning from his corner noticed a large manila folder in the stash house's mail box; it was addressed to Alfonso Lewis. He took it to Sunshine's office where he knocked on the closed door. A voice asked who's there. "Little Bit." Come in,

"What can I do for you, Little Bit?" Asked Sunshine.

"Good morning, Mr. Lewis, I found this envelope in the mail box and thought I would bring it to you. I hope you don't mind my interrupting you."

"Absolutely not."

Little Bit handed the large envelope to Sunshine, who thanked him. Little Bit walked out of the office to find Marcus to vent about a problem he was having with another street boy.

Sunshine saw the date and time stamp on the envelope; it had been sent from New York. In it was a hand-written letter from Slice, writing to tell Sunshine Cedrica's parents had been killed execution style in prison by the Colombian cartel, who was relentless when it came to punishing those who crossed it as the Smiths had done. The New York group lost the money it gave the Smiths for the drugs, but the Colombians had still not been paid for the drugs, which the police in the Caymans was believed to have confiscated. Both groups seemingly had lost big-time.

Slice was warning Sunshine, since he and White Chocolate were the last to be seen associating with the Smiths, maybe they had been given the money due the cartel. Sunshine knew nothing about the money Slice was referring to or where it might be.

Soon after that, Sunshine started getting death threats from Latino groups on the West Side. Apparently, they had ties to the Colombian cartel and were harassing Sunshine and his group on the cartel's behalf. As the Latinos continued their harassment, the Black Gangster groups in the area including the Almighty Black P. Stone Nation, Vice Lord Nation, Folk Nation, and the Gangster Disciples circled their wagons to protect their market and a brother, Sunshine.

The Latinos working the mean streets were looking for any information they could find about Sunshine, his association with the New York group, and ties to the Smiths. The Colombian drug cartel would stop at nothing until fully compensated one way or other. Slice and Sunshine had to tread lightly and carry big sticks if they wanted to survive. It was a silent but deadly game being played out between two tarnished factions.

The Latinos' concerted action lasted weeks, but found no connection between Sunshine and the Smiths or any indication where the money might be. After a while, the Latinos backed off their annoying harassment and returned to business as usual. But Sunshine knew it was not over. The Colombians were determined and merciless and stop at nothing to find the lost cash.

Sunshine now more distraught than ever. Troubled with the drug business, realizing he had to find another calling. He'd been thinking of becoming a paid informant for the FBI or CIA since his involvement in most aspects of the drug business and money laundering. Familiar with the ins and outs of the business and ready to join forces to put a stop to the killing and maiming associated with gang violence and drugs.

He was not getting younger, and had to face reality sometime. It was time to consider his daughters as well as White Chocolate and their dreams of the future. The thought of his daughters growing up in a turbulent and uncontrollable neighborhood was not acceptable. He spent much of his life being an integral part committing those vicious actions which ran contrary to society's concept. It was time to move on for their daughters' sake.

He put the word out to several of his contacts in law enforcement and city officials about his intent. It did not take long before he piqued the interest of several intelligence agencies including the Drug Enforcement Agency, the DEA, which investigates drug and money-laundering business.

After being interviewed several times by different departments of the agency, Agent Goodfellow had Sunshine come to his office one morning and told him, "I'm hiring you as a confidential informant strictly on the basis of your ability to provide information that will help us with search and seizures of drugs and money being laundered in and around Chicago."

It did not take Sunshine and White Chocolate long to disassociate themselves from the drug business.

When Sunshine told Marcus of his plans and offered Marcus the business. Marcus told him, "The drug business is the only life I've ever known. I love the excitement, power, and money. I have no interest in leaving the drug trade. With no family, only myself to look after, I'm happy to continue in this rough and rocky business of selling drugs as usual with the group I'm all too familiar with." He would continue doing what he did best and accept the risk because of the money and power it offered.

Sunshine was ready to hit the streets as a CI collecting information on local drug dealers, traffickers, and money launderers. His first several weeks working undercover for DEA did not turn out well, however, for him or the DEA. He had been involved with a small but notorious group of Mexicans on the South Side, in Little Village, which sold its services to any cartel or group willing to pay the price. They were involved in killings, drug smuggling, and money laundering.

Sunshine spent time hanging around and worming his way into the group; he wanted to gain its members' confidence and learn as much about their operation as possible.

One day, he heard through the grapevine that a local policeman on the take mentioned to someone high up in the organization that he recognized Sunshine. Sunshine immediately dropped out of sight to regroup. It was the only choice he had if he didn't want to be identified as a mole.

The next day, Sunshine headed in the opposite direction, downtown, where he was less known and able in continuing his snooping for the DEA. Working a new neighborhood was not easy; it took time for him to gain the confidence of a new group of corner boys who could introduce him to the higher-ups they worked for.

After a couple of months of nosing around and asking the right questions, Sunshine finally got his first real break. One afternoon, he was sitting alone having lunch when a man approached him and asked, "Would you mind if I join you since there seems to be no other seating available?"

"Sure, have a seat. I'd enjoy the company."

"Thank you. Don't think I've seen this restaurant so crowded, and I've been coming here for years. Don't think I've seen you before either. Do you come here often?"

"Yes, a couple of times a week but only when I'm downtown. I seem to recall seeing you a time or two when I've come in."

The man reached across the table to shake Sunshine's hand. "My name's DeShawn Adams."

"Glad to meet you. I'm Alfonso Lewis."

Meeting by chance that day at the restaurant had been a million-to-one shot, a huge score for Sunshine and the DEA. He had just met a kingpin, a man in charge of a major group working the downtown district and the entire East Side of Chicago, a real find. Their first meeting started off rather casually, but it turned out to be more informative than Sunshine had hoped for. They hit it off and became friends of sorts that day.

They met several times at that restaurant, as DeShawn slowly began letting his guard down as he became more familiar with Sunshine. In time, DeShawn indicated in increments to Sunshine the line of work he was involved with.

One day, he asked Sunshine, "Would you be interested in working for me? I could use your expertise in my organization." DeShawn was hooked. Sunshine had revealed enough of his background DeShawn was ready to take him aboard. He had conversed with Sunshine enough to learn he was well versed in the drug and money-laundering business, and able to carry on a functional conversation about that business, had impressed DeShawn.

Sunshine slowly learned DeShawn was involved in selling and servicing drug cartels throughout the Midwest; he did it all—smuggling and transporting drugs and laundering drug money. It was a more sophisticated and dangerous operation than Sunshine ever expected to be involved in. Sunshine considered DeShawn a major player way above the nickel-and-dime stuff Sunshine had been involved with. DeShawn's game was certainly not for the faint of heart but just what the DEA was expecting Sunshine to connect with and rat out.

"I'll give it some thought and get back to you soon," Sunshine told him. He had to run DeShawn's offer past the DEA first before committing.

Sunshine's answer did not set well with DeShawn. He quickly told Sunshine before leaving, "I'll need your answer in the next day or so or the offer is off the table."

Sunshine agreed he would get back with his answer as soon as possible.

That afternoon, he went to DEA headquarters to inform Goodfellow about the proposition this DeShawn fellow had proposed and what he had learned about the man's business.

Goodfellow told Sunshine, "I'll talk it over with some of the other agents and get their take on what you've told me and what we need you to do."

A half hour later, Goodfellow returned to his office and told Sunshine, "We've decided to let you go undercover and work with DeShawn's organization. I'm letting you know up front that we'll deny any knowledge of you if anything happens and your cover is blown.

"We've been aware of DeShawn Adams for some time but not what his position in the organization was until now. He appeared to be just another low-level drug dealer, but based on what you've told us, we need to expose him and his organization for what it really is. It would mean so much to the country, not just Chicago. DEA's sole purpose is to eradicate such groups. If you think you can become embedded in the organization and pull this caper off, go for it. The agency will back you as far as our limitations will allow."

CHAPTER 16

Sunshine left Goodfellow's office feeling overwhelmed by what he just volunteered for. The job would require him to walk a tightrope without a safety net. It would not be easy penetrating such a sophisticated operation while hiding his connection with the DEA as a CI. He had to play his cards close to his chest every minute he was around DeShawn and not flinch when talking or being questioned about his past. He had to be upfront with everything he had done until his involvement with the DEA. He knew he'd have to say as little as possible and learn as much as he could about the operation. His world hung in the balance between what he said and did. He had to make the best of a bad situation to simply survive.

Sunshine was strong and had the stamina and resilience; he knew he would succeed if he played his cards right. He was good at most things he set his mind to do. This was just one more endeavor on his journey to help clean up the felonious activities he helped establish over the years. He was doing this primarily for White Chocolate and their daughters. He wanted them to have what he had never had, a chance to live the good life, not the one he had growing up. He knew there was a better way to live that didn't involve having to constantly look over one's shoulder in fear, and he wanted that for his family.

The next day, Sunshine was arrived early to meet DeShawn at the restaurant. DeShawn came in and spotted him at a table for two along the back wall. He walked back to where Sunshine sat, and asked before sitting down, "Are you going to accept my offer?"

"I've talked it over with my girlfriend. She's agreed the change would be good for me. If your offer still stands, I'm more than happy to accept your proposition."

"Good. You've made the right choice. DeShawn sat down and told Sunshine, "After lunch we'll go back to my office, I'll introduce you the rest of my associates."

After lunch, DeShawn picked up the check, and the two of them walked outside. DeShawn pointed to his car and told Sunshine, "Follow me back to the office."

Sunshine had parked down the street. DeShawn waited until he saw Sunshine pull out before he pulled away from the curb.

DeShawn led Sunshine to the building where his office was located. Before entering the parking garage, DeShawn motioned to Sunshine to park in the visitors' parking area alongside the building. DeShawn drove into the garage and soon emerged back outside where he motioned Sunshine to follow him, and the two walked through the revolving door and onto the elevator.

Inside the elevator, DeShawn said, "My office is on the top floor. Great view of Lake Michigan." Think you'll be impressed.

When the elevator doors opened, Sunshine admired the magnificent view and thought, *I'm in awe. It's beyond description. Furnished like in the movies. How can anyone afford such a palatial place?*

"Follow me," DeShawn said.

They passed the secretary's desk, as DeShawn stopped and spoke to her. "Myriam, this is Mr. Alfonso Lewis, the newest member of our firm. He'll be assisting me in certain aspects of the business. If there's anything he needs, I'd appreciate your doing what you can to help him."

"Glad to make your acquaintance, Mr. Lewis," Myriam said standing up and offering Sunshine her hand.

"Likewise, I'm sure," Sunshine replied as the two shook hands.

DeShawn admired Sunshine's tone and manners.

"Let's go to my office. I have a few things I need to discuss with you before you get started. There's a lot to learn about the organization and I need you to get up to speed as quickly as possible."

"I'll do my best."

Reaching DeShawn's office, DeShawn walked over to his desk and riffled through the top drawer; as he retrieved a folder, he reached over handing it to Sunshine. "You'll need to memorize everything in this folder. You must understand the firm's guidelines as they pertain to you and follow them without question. Only certain aspects of the business require your involvement. Other components of the organization run entirely independently and considered stand-alone entities. The department I'm assigning you to has been departmentalized as a single, functioning, cohesive element by itself. You're not to talk to anyone outside this office about what goes on behind closed doors, understood?"

"Yes, I get your point. I'll abide by the guidelines and its rules."

DeShawn led Sunshine out of his office and down a hallway lined with offices. He said, "Only on occasion will you meet other employees and then only on a need-to-know basis."

DeShawn led Sunshine to a small office located at the end of the hallway next to a stairwell. A cracker box compared to offices they had passed on the way; it was not what he expected. It had no windows overlooking Lake Michigan, and no bigger than a broom closet, but adequate, he would make do.

"First, acquaint yourself with what's inside the folder, memorize it in its entirety. I'll see you tomorrow morning, at which time we'll discuss your job description."

Sunshine sat at his small but adequate desk. which took up a large part of the room. He began by opening the folder and started reading the contents of the folder. He could not believe what he was reading. He began to see the handwriting on the wall. His new job would be difficult, but he was determined to help stop the corruption and exploitation by people like DeShawn, who deal in all sorts of illegal activities, 24/7.

He quickly learned DeShawn's organization was more complex and multifaceted than he realized. Sunshine, at his point had to tread softly; the script he'd been handed was going to be difficult at best to follow, as he now had to prepare mentally and physically for the challenges that lay ahead. Thinking again to himself, *what have I gotten myself into? Did*

I sign up to help rid the city of its illicit and criminal aspect or for my own satisfaction? A little of both, he thought out loud.

He knew he had not been on the straight and narrow for many years. He knew he made the right choice joining forces with the DEA, but now felt he had a big bulls'-eye on his back. He couldn't afford to make mistakes if he wanted to bring down DeShawn.

After his first day he left his small office and headed home to White Chocolate, Queenetta, and Cedrica. He needed to enjoyed quality time with family.

He told White Chocolate after arriving home, "My job for DeShawn is as a bag man. But my real work will be distributing disinformation to one side while supplying critical information to the other side." He said, trying to reinforced his decision about working for the DEA.

After dinner, he supervised the girls' brushing their teeth and getting ready for bed. After tucking them in, White Chocolate came upstairs having washed the dishes and cleaning the kitchen. Sunshine told her, "it's been a long day, and I'm ready to hit the hay." But he had a hard time falling asleep. His mind was going a hundred miles a minute as he thought to himself, *if I get fingered as a DEA plant in DeShawn's den of wolves, my life is over.* He also asked himself, *do I really have the tenacity* to *carry out this obligation,* realizing if he did, it would signify in some small way, he had done something right by contribute back to society, rather than tearing the fabric of society apart.

As he was going over such thoughts in his mind, the phone rang. He reached over picked up the phone and answered it.

"Hello?"

"Alfonso, this is DeShawn. I need you to meet a courier later this evening and pick up a package, bring it with you to the office tomorrow. The courier will be at the North Western Railway Kinzie Street Bridge on the north end of the Chicago *Sun-Times* building. Get there no later than ten thirty. If you see or are suspicious of any unusual activity near the drop, do not, and I repeat, do not stick around. We'll schedule it for a later date. See you tomorrow morning."

White Chocolate looked worried. "What was that all about?"

He told her it was DeShawn and he had a job for him later that evening. This did not sit well with her. They both wondered if this would become the family's new norm—not knowing what to expect from moment to moment, night or day. That would definitely put a strain on their relationship, which was frayed and tattered by all that's happened to them lately.

"I'm worried about what could happen this evening downtown," she said. "You and I both know that area by Kinzie Street Bridge is a dangerous place. It's where a lot of the lowlifes hang out, and evil lurks around every corner. Not one of the better places to go for a stroll late at night."

"How well I know, but I'll be careful. Don't worry. That's where the drop takes place. It's part of my job for DeShawn and the DEA, which needs a good inside CI. You understood that going in."

"I do, but this intelligence gathering you're doing is dangerous. I worry about if you'll be coming home afterwards." Just looking out for your best interest. "Yes, and I appreciate your concern."

"I'm sorry it's come to this, but don't want to be late for my first assignment," he said with a chuckle. "I don't know what time I'll be home, but if you're asleep, I'll wake you up and let you know how things went." He wanted her to know it should be just a typical drop-off and pickup scenario. At least that's what he was hoping it would be.

She looked at him with trepidation.

Sunshine got dressed, kissed White Chocolate before leaving the room. Once he was outside, opened the car door, crawled behind the wheel and drove off as he headed toward downtown and the Kinzie Street Bridge area to pick up either drugs or money; he didn't know which, he didn't need to know just retrieve the package and take it to work the following morning. He would do whatever it was Deshawn asked him to do. He arrived in the area and drove around spotting what looked like the drop-off site. He spotted a car half a block away, parked in a no-parking zone. He drove slowly toward the car until he saw the car was occupied. About that time someone in the car signaled with a brief flash of light indicating that's where the exchange was to take place. Sunshine pulled slowly up alongside, when who was inside rolled down the driver's window, handing Sunshine a small bag, and immediately drove off.

Sunshine put the bag down on the passenger's seat and drove away thinking, *that was a piece of cake.*

When all of a sudden, all hell broke loose.

He was quickly surrounded by several police cars with red lights flashing. He stopped. Several police officers with guns drawn approached his car. He did not know what the hell was happening. As one of the officers approached his car, said in a threatening voice, "Step out of the car slowly with your hands high above your head. Now!"

Sunshine opened his door and eased out of the car with hands held high. Several other officers in the meantime grabbed him and threw him up against his car; and one of the officers pulled his arms down and cuffed him. Then frisked him while he was spread eagle over the hood of his car. Finding nothing, he put Sunshine in the back of one of the squad cars, while others police on scene searched his car, finding the bag, which the police assumed was a drop bag. They put it on the trunk of Sunshine's car.

One of the officers walked over to the car where Sunshine sat shackled and asked, "Why were you driving around down here tonight? Did you know the person in the car who gave you this bag and would you mind if we looked in it?"

"Do I have a choice?"

"Not really. We'll find out eventually. And by the way who do you work for?"

Sunshine's answer was the standard response given by anyone caught red-handed in such a bust: "I was just out for a late-night drive. And no, I didn't know who was in the other car. He handed me personal property; you have no right to search the bag. And I'm not employed."

The officer returned to Sunshine's car and unzipped the bag. To his surprise, he found only a few pieces of dirty clothing. Their takedown had been for naught. He zipped the bag up and took it to the patrol car in which Sunshine was sitting. The officer opened the door and told

Sunshine to step out. After he did, the officer uncuffed him. "Sorry for the delay. You're free to go."

"Why did you stop and detain me in the first place?" Sunshine asked as if he were innocent.

The officer in charge said, "We were informed that someone would be here this evening to pick up a large amount of drugs or money. When we saw you drive up and witnessed some sort of exchange, we assumed it was the drop we were expecting. But it turned out to be a dry run. You keep doing this and we'll catch you red-handed one day and throw the book at you. Don't want to see you back down here again, understand?"

Sunshine drove home a bit shaken but wiser for the experience. *Have I made a mistake by taking on such a dangerous undertaking?* He asked himself.

Back home, he woke up White Chocolate and told her of his harrowing experience. She was glad he had not been shot or arrested.

The next morning, DeShawn met Sunshine as he walked into the lobby. He had been waiting to get Sunshine's feedback about the pseudo drop. The courier told DeShawn about the drop earlier. Explained to DeShawn, "I saw several patrol cars in the drop location and decided to switch drop bags and hand off the decoy bag." Luckily for you, he did or you would have been arrested for delivery of a controlled substance or dirty money.

DeShawn told Sunshine, "Follow me to my office," As they arrived inside the office, DeShawn looked over at Sunshine and told him, "Put the bag on my desk." Sunshine laid the bag on the desk and took a seat in one of the leather chairs near DeShawn's desk. DeShawn walked around his desk and sat down, immediately pulling the bag across the desk. When he had it in front of him, he unzipped the decoy bag. As he did, DeShawn saw what was inside and smiled over at Sunshine and told him, "I'm glad the fast-thinking courier spotted those patrol cars staking out the area. He saved both me and you a big headache. I want to hear your side of the story from beginning to end. With both of your inputs, maybe I can learn something that will benefit me in future drops."

"Sure. As I approached the drop area near the Kinzie Street Bridge, I looked around to see if I could spot anything suspicious but saw nothing out of the ordinary. There were no cop cars or suspicious individuals wandering the streets. The area around the drop area was deserted. The drop itself went down without a hitch, but as I was leaving, several police cars appeared out of nowhere with their lights and sirens blaring. I was surrounded before I knew what was happening. If you ask me, I think we were set up."

"Did anyone else have knowledge of the drop site besides you, the courier, and me?"

"No. Not that I know of."

"What did the police say after they detained you and opened up the bag of dirty clothes?"

"One told me, 'This is your lucky day, Lewis,' and removed me from the car and uncuffed me. With a smirk on his face, he handed me back the bag and said, 'You're free to go. Without any hard evidence, I guess there's nothing we can do but let you walk.'"

"So, what do you think? Do you suspect you were set up? "Yes. How did anyone know I would be there at that time?"

Who do you thing told them?" DeShawn asked.

"I don't have the foggiest idea, but somehow, someone heard about the drop and informed the police. It was too easy not to have been a setup."

DeShawn, now upset told Sunshine, "I got to find out who's tipping off the police. They need to be silenced. Ask around and see if you can get a handle on the unidentified informant. I don't need this kind of interruption from outsiders. We'll try again tomorrow night. I'll make sure this time it goes off without a hitch."

"I'll keep my eyes and ears open. Maybe I'll run across the snitch or someone who knows him. I'll let you know. I've had some experience in the past of tracking down informants."

"Good. With everyone in the association looking, we should be able to trace him or her down in short order. Be careful who you talk to, but let me know if you hear anything about a possible snitch within or outside the organization. When and if we find him, I'm going to have the SOB castrated."

CHAPTER 17

During his lunch break that afternoon, Sunshine called Goodfellow from a pay phone down the street from his office. He told the agent all about his harrowing experience the previous night. He told him DeShawn was upset and put out the word out he wanted to hear from anyone with information or knowledge of a snitch.

"Is there anything I can do differently next time?" Sunshine asked. "If I'm arrested, I don't want DeShawn to know that I'm the snitch helping to set him up. DeShawn told me there would be another attempt at a drop tomorrow night, but hasn't yet told me when or where. Guess he's keeping it under wraps until time for the drop. Doesn't want any screwups."

"As soon as you learn the location and time, call me. I'll have someone on scene before the drop goes down and follow the courier after the drop. If we're lucky, we might learn where the courier lives and where and how he makes his pickups prior to delivery. The more we learn of DeShawn's operation, the better we can do our job. Keep up the good work, but don't get brave and blow your cover. Keep in contact when possible, and continue keeping a low profile."

Sunshine returned to work after lunch, as he passed Myriam's desk, she handed him a large manila envelope. He looked at the manila envelope, back to her, thanking her. Back in his office, he studied it carefully before opening. It contained no return address, which was strange, and nothing indicating where it had come from or who sent it. Curiosity got the best of him. He eventually opened the envelope and found a hand-printed note, a map, and two AFAIK plane tickets—a one-way to Grand

Cayman and a second ticket to Little Cayman. The note contained instructions about what he was to do once he returned to the Grand Caymans. *Who sent me a one-way ticket back to Grand Cayman? I thought I'd seen the last of that island.* As he studied the contents that were inside.

Once he got over the initial shock, he realized he had to call Goodfellow about this and find out what he wanted him to do.

Later that afternoon, he made up an excuse to leave the office. He once again headed to the pay phone where he called Agent Goodfellow about the new development. Goodfellow was surprised as Sunshine had been receiving the envelope. He asked Sunshine, "Any idea who it is or why they want you to return to the Caymans?"

"Not a clue."

"Someone's serious about wanting you to back. Go and find out what this is all about. It may be the break we've been waiting for, a real chance to bust up the Colombia cartel. Get ready to go. I'll have our agent there keep you under constant surveillance. He's one of most respected and responsible agents in the Caribbean. He'll have your back at all times. Just remember, be careful. Don't jeopardize your cover. If you do, you could be in real danger.

"Tell DeShawn something has come up and you have to leave the country for a few days on a personal matter. If he gets too personal, just tell him you can't divulge what the matter entails. If he continues questioning you, tell him it's a matter of life or death. I'm sure he'll get the message."

Sunshine was worried about going to the Caymans; his last two trips there had been filled with enough drama and intrigue to last a lifetime. Arriving back at the office, he went directly to DeShawn's office and knocked on the door. "Come in!" he heard DeShawn say.

He entered and asked, "Can I have a word with you?"

"Sure. What's on your mind?"

Sunshine felt he was in a Catch-22. He explained to DeShawn that he had to leave the country on some personal business. After what seemed an eternity, DeShawn said, "I'm not in favor of your leaving the country and leaving me shorthanded. If it's a matter you must attend to, go, but I expect you back as soon as you finish your business."

DeShawn knew Sunshine would not have asked for time off if it had not been important.

When Sunshine got home that evening, he told White Chocolate about the note, and the plane tickets. She was as surprised as Sunshine was getting an anonymous manila envelope delivered to his office rather than at home.

"Agent Goodfellow told me to go and see where it leads." He said the agent in the Caymans would shadow me while there. He wants me to debrief me as soon as I get back. He said he would alert the local drug enforcement agency in the area about my trip; they'll try and help me in case of an emergency. He wants me to journal my activities and contacts so nothing is lost when I return and debriefed.

He said, "the DEA has a good rapport with the Cayman DEA because of all the illegal drug activities in and around the Caymans and the Caribbean which most of the traffic originates out of Colombia and several other countries. He gave me a phone number and name to call if I need assistance from law enforcement or the DEA. He told me to be careful and wished me good luck."

His flight was to leave the following morning. White Chocolate helped him pack that evening. He wanted to get this over with and behind him as soon as possible.

At breakfast the next morning, he told White Chocolate, "Be careful while I'm away. I'll miss you and the kids." After kissing her cheek, he left for the airport in his car.

Reaching the airport, and parking his car in one of the long-term lots knowing he would be away for more than a couple of days. He took the shuttle to the main terminal straight to the check-in counter. He gave the clerk his one-way ticket to the Grand Caymans.

She asked, "Do you have duffle bag you would like checked in?"

Sunshine put his duffle bag on the scale, and the counter clerk attached a checked baggage claim ticket to it and handed back his boarding pass along with a baggage claim ticket. Then proceeded to the departure gate where he was told, "Your plane will be boarding soon, Mr. Lewis, have your boarding pass handy when you reach the boarding area."

When his flight was announced, he got in line at gate 23. As he proceeded through the line, he noticed a somewhat familiar face behind him. He did not acknowledge the person, but wondered why whoever it was being discreet when Sunshine tried making eye contact. This was not Sunshine's first rodeo; he sensed he was being followed but didn't know by whom or why. Sunshine felt a sense of intrigue, but he was also cautious. *Friend or foe? Someone sent to watch me for my own good or not for my own good? Time will tell.*

Arriving on Grand Cayman brought back bad memories of this godforsaken Island he swore after leaving the last time that he'd never to return.

Even though it had been a couple of years since his last visit, his name remained on the country's active file as someone to be scrutinized closely before being allowed entry. He was red-flagged immediately and pulled aside, and escorted to a separate room inside the terminal.

A customs official told him to take off his shoes and clothes down to his underwear. As he complied with the request, another customs official was emptying his duffle bag on a counter and examining its contents. Customs officials before finishing questioned him about his visit and where he was staying while on the island. He gave them what he could but he himself had no idea about where he would be or be staying.

Sunshine happened to be looking out the small window in the door when spotted the stranger going through customs and quickly disappear. After being searched and his baggage examined, he was cleared through customs to continue his trip.

Once outside the terminal, he was met immediately by a contact who quickly hustled him off in a cab to a hotel and was told to stay there until morning, when the contact would return to drive him to the airport for his flight to Little Cayman.

The following morning, Sunshine received a call; the cab was on its way to pick him up and drive him to the airport. His flight to Little Cayman was scheduled for departure at nine.

Sunshine was waiting outside along with his duffle bag waiting as the cab pulled up. The driver stopped the car and got out, walked around back of the car and opened the trunk. Then took Sunshine's duffle bag, and put it inside the trunk and closed the lid.

He told Sunshine, "Get in."

On the way to the airport, the driver looked in the rearview mirror and said in broken English, "Once yuzu's on Little Cayman, yuzus be contacted byes a go-between who's will brief yuzus on what's yuzu's gonna do next."

The secrecy was getting too much for Sunshine, who felt he had no control over his life at this time.

In the terminal, he saw a prop plane taxi up to the terminal. *This must be my puddle jumper which will take me to Little Cayman.*

The announcement came over the PA system: "AFAIK flight 404 has just landed. After dropping off passengers and refueling, we will commence boarding. Please have your boarding passes ready."

It was not long before the departure gate became active; those with tickets for Little Cayman were checked through and walked out onto the tarmac and boarded the twin-engine prop plane. After everyone was onboard the DHC-6-4, the flight attendant said, "Welcome aboard AFAIK Airlines flight 404, destination, Little Cayman Island. Please secure your seat belts. Remain in your seat at all times and relax for the short flight to Little Cayman."

After that, the passengers were briefed on what to do if the plane developed a problem and ditch itself in the water.

It was now the Captains time to make his brief announcement over the PA system. He began by a cheerful, "Good morning, ladies and gentlemen. My name is Captain Jerry Hornbeck. I'll be your pilot along with my copilot, Lieutenant Randy Johnson, for our short flight to Little Cayman. The weather report indicates a perfect day for flying—clear skies and balmy. Please sit back enjoy the view and enjoy your trip."

After arriving on Little Cayman, Sunshine was met by another contact, who drove him to Sam McCoy's Lodge. It had been a much larger place prior to being hit by a hurricane that had destroyed most of the lodging a few years earlier. It was more of a watering hole, a small bar on the beach, than a resort. A sign in the window read, Open at Noon. It was only eleven thirty.

He decided to scope out the area and see what else this place had to offer. As he ambled up and down the beach looking for any signs of life, he heard an outboard engine getting louder and louder as he waited with bated breath. He spotted a small boat heading in his direction. He wondered, *What's the purpose of this trip? Who's behind it? And what am I doing here? Too many questions. Too few answers.*

The pilot of the small outboard boat cut the engine, and let the forward momentum of the boat drifted slowly up to the beach. A tall, dark stranger with dreadlocks motioned to him to come closer to the water's edge and told him to take off his shoes and socks and roll up his pant legs. Sunshine did so and waded out in the shallow water to the boat. Pitching his duffle bag in the boat and help from the stranger climbed aboard. Without fanfare, the stranger returned to his seat and started the engine. He slowly backed the boat away from the beach, until it reached deeper water, turned the boat in the direction of open water, heading back in the direction he came from.

A half hour later, Sunshine saw a larger craft on the horizon rocking back and forth as if awaiting his arrival. He saw someone standing alongside the railing on the aft deck, someone he believed he recognized. The closer they came to the drifting vessel, the easier it was for Sunshine to make out who it was and put two and two together. *Who else but Captain Eubanks, chief of police? But why is he waiting for me in the middle of the Caribbean Sea?* Another question without an answer.

Sunshine climbed up the short ladder hanging off the side of the vessel and on to the aft deck. Once aboard Captain Eubanks casually welcomed him aboard. He smiled at Sunshine and seemed rather happy to see him again.

"Did you have a pleasant flight and boat ride?"

"Yes, to both questions, but I'm unsure of why I'm here."

"I'll explain everything in due time," Captain Eubanks said.

After Sunshine was seated and somewhat relaxed, he was provided with food and drink.

"Mr. Lewis, we're still working on the Smiths' case and need to know what you and your partner knew about their drug operation. Do you have any idea what happened to the money they had? Since you and your partner were the last ones seen with them before their arrest, I thought maybe you've had time to reflect on what transpired during that short period you were in their presence. Did they say anything to you about the money they were carrying? Would you have any inkling of where they might have stashed it before being arrested?

"I've learned the cartel in Colombia was pulling out all the stops to recover their money the Smiths absconded with. I'm assuming you or your companion had information as to where the money might be. We need to find it before things gets totally out of hand on your end and ours."

"Captain Eubanks, we weren't that close to the Smiths. We met them a day or two before we were to head back to Chicago."

"In those couple of days, did they discuss what their line of business was, and were you ever asked to become involved?"

"They received a call from Slice in New York concerning the drugs they were carrying. Slice suggested they ask us if we would be interested in delivering the shipment as we returned to Chicago.

"What did you tell them?"

"I told them I wasn't interested, risking being caught, spending the rest of my life in prison. Leroy thought I would do them a favor by bringing the drugs back, but I told him I wasn't interested and the subject was dropped." As far as talking with the Smiths later concerning the drugs, you had already arrested them.

Later, I was contacted Slice working out of New York. He told me the New York syndicate had gotten word from the Colombian cartel that the Smiths had been detained on drug charges and the cartel had not been paid.

"Do you remember any time when you saw Mr. Smith carrying

around an extra bag or backpack? Like when you went with them to the farm on that excursion?"

"Yes, now that you mention it. Leroy always wore a small, black backpack. I don't remember seeing him without it, but I never gave it much thought."

"We think it held the money owed to the drug cartel for the drugs. That's why he never let the backpack out of his sight. Did he have it on the day of the trip to the farm?"

"I think he was wearing it when we left the bus for our guided tour of the farm and cave, but don't recall seeing it after we returned to the bus for our trip back to town."

"I appreciate your honesty, Mr. Lewis. Tomorrow, you'll be flying back to Grand Cayman, and were going to take a trip to the farm to see if maybe he left it there. Until then, enjoy the surroundings. If there's anything my crew or I can do to make your trip more enjoyable, let us know."

After dinner that night, Sunshine asked to be excused; he went below to shower and freshen up before going to bed. He had had a long day and was worn out, but so many questions were racing through his mind. *Why did Captain Eubanks fly me down here with all this secrecy? Is he involved with the Colombian cartel? How else could he afford this vessel and lifestyle on his salary from the police department? Things aren't adding up. He seems available at a moment's notice to intervene in any situation concerning the cartel. Is he playing both sides against the middle and keeping his hands in the mix while keeping both sides in check?*

Early next morning, Sunshine heard the twin diesels fire up and the anchor clattering as it was pulled up. He crawled out of the bed, dressed, and headed to the aft deck, where Eubanks was drinking coffee and smoking a large Cuban cigar. The captain waved him over, and Sunshine took a seat at his table. The captain offered him some freshly brewed Colombian coffee. As they sat drinking their coffee, the yacht began moving and appeared to be heading back to Little Cayman. A little while later, the yacht pulled alongside the dock in front of McCoy's.

Captain Eubanks explained to Sunshine, "You're being dropped off.

A taxi will be arriving soon to take you to catch a plane back to Grand Cayman. The driver will give you a ticket. You'll be met at the airport and taken to a hotel. You'll stay there until you're contacted. In a day or two, I'll pick you up, and we'll return to the farm to see if we can locate that backpack Mr. Smith was carrying when he visited the farm."

By then, Sunshine had concluded that Eubanks was deeply involved in the Colombian cartel. *Why else would he have gone to such lengths to get me back here and help him find the money? Maybe he has plans for the money himself.*

Sunshine thought it would be a miracle if the money suddenly turned up after all that time. He was sure someone would have found it, maybe a tourist visiting the farm. They might never know what happened to it. The trip was turning into such a clandestine undertaking, so unbelievable and too farfetched to comprehend.

CHAPTER 18

A couple of days later, Sunshine heard a knock on his hotel room door. He got up and peered through the peephole; it was Captain Eubanks and two of his officers standing in the hall. Sunshine opened the door and invited them in.

Captain Eubanks shook Sunshine's hand and said, "If you're ready, it's time to go to the farm."

"I'm ready. I hope you can find that backpack because I'm ready to return to Chicago. I'm sure you understand. Do I have time to grab a donut and a coffee before we go? I haven't had breakfast."

"We can stop at the breakfast bar on our way out. It might be a long time before you get to eat again."

The phone rang. Sunshine asked, "Do you mind if I answer it?"

"No. We have to get to the farm. Whoever it is will call back or leave a message."

Stopping at the breakfast bar on their way out, Sunshine grabbed a quick bite. He was then hustled to an unmarked car parked under the portico.

It did not take long to drive out to the farm. The foursome exited the car and headed to the farmhouse. Captain Eubanks knocked on the door, when this rather large man opened the door and asked, "To what do I owe this pleasure, Captain Eubanks?"

"I'm here on a drug investigation we've been working on for a couple of years. It's come to our attention the last place the couple involved in the investigation visited was your farm. I'm asking your permission to access the cave. We're following a lead that the couple might have stashed some sort of backpack in it."

"You're telling me someone might have left something in the cave? Can't believe that. I've been in that cave many times in the past year or so and don't recall seeing anything matching that description."

"We'd like to check ourselves with your permission of course. If we're lucky enough to find the backpack, my department and I would be eternally grateful to you. The party to whom the contents belong is anxious for its return. I think they'd want to reward you generously if the property was returned. I can't tell you what we're looking for or what's inside the backpack since it's an ongoing investigation. I'm sure you understand."

"No, not really, but go look around. If I can help you, just let me know."

"I will. And one more favor. Would you be so kind as to have Miguel saddle four horses?"

"Sure. Let me get hold of Miguel. In fact, I'll have him ride along so you don't get lost."

"Thank you. It shouldn't take long for us to check the cave out."

Miguel saddled up the horses. As they mounted up, Sunshine sensed that the captain was almost giddy at the idea of finding the backpack and getting a reward from the cartel or perhaps keeping it for himself.

On their way out to the cave site, Sunshine thought about his previous trip to the cave two years earlier. Sunshine remembered Leroy leaving the group and riding off over the rocks to a single tree by a boulder to relieve himself. Sunshine couldn't remember if Leroy had had the backpack once he rejoined the group or not. He thought, *If Leroy had had the backpack with him when we entered the cave, he would have had to take it off to squeeze through the narrow entrance.*

The four arrived at the entrance to the cave where they dismounted. Being a large man, Captain Eubanks himself was barely able squeezing through the narrow opening but managed somehow. Once inside the cave, the four spread out searching every nook and cranny but came up empty-handed at the end. Captain Eubanks after satisfying his curiosity that the backpack was not inside the cave. After their intensive search, decided it was time to stop searching for the infamous backpack and head back to the farm.

As Sunshine once again passed the lone tree by the large boulder near the trail, the certainty what he would find if able to visit that site was his positivity. Determined to check the spot before leaving the Island to satisfy his own curiosity if nothing else, it was worth a look. He decided at that moment passing by the tree and rock to return for a closer look-see tomorrow.

After returning to the police station, Captain Eubanks told Sunshine, "You'll be able to return to Chicago in a couple of days once I fill out my report and go over your story once more. I'll need you to stick around here a little longer in case further information in this matter requires additional inquiry. I'm sure you can relate to my Catch-22 and appreciate the situation I too am in."

Captain Eubanks had exhausted all his ideas about where the money had been hidden. Even the elaborate meeting on Captains Eubanks boat and in-depth interview had not turned up anything new or useful. Captain Eubanks was between a rock and a hard place contemplating how to get back into the good graces of the cartel after exhausting all avenues at his disposal and coming up empty handed.

It was now Monday. Sunshine's room was at the hotel was let until Thursday, plenty of time in returning to the farm and checking out his intuition about the tree and boulder. As he entered the hotel, he walked over to the concierge office and told him he wanted to signed up for the farm tour the following day.

That Tuesday morning, Sunshine along with a dozen other tourists took the tour bus back out to the farm. On the ride to the cave, he had only one thing on his mind—that backpack. If he found the backpack, once back intown he planned on making a beeline to his bank making a large deposit to his account.

At the farm, Miguel gave the group his usual orientation, prior to the group mounting up. Once on their way, Sunshine's only thought was about how he was going to excuse himself from the group and make a detour out to the tree and large boulder. His thought was to ask Miguel permission to stop on the return trip from the cave to take a photo of the spot. He knew the tourists would not give him a second thought or look when he cut off the trail and headed for the tree and boulder. Finding the backpack would change his life, and this seemed to be his last chance.

After the group left the cave and, on the way, back to the farm; Sunshine rode up alongside Miguel and said, "Last time I was here with my friend, she wanted a photo of the unusual lone tree near the huge boulder. Said it would be the perfect picture to enlarge, frame, and hang in our living room back home. It would be a reminder or memento of our trip to the Grand Caymans. Would you mind if I hustle over there for a close up shot while I'm here? It would mean everything to the little lady if know what I mean?"

"Okay, but try not to be too long. The bus will be waiting to drive you to town when we arrive back at the farm house."

"Thanks, I won't be long."

As they approached the spot where Sunshine was to veer off the trail away from the group, Miguel gave him a nod. Sunshine cut his horse to the right and off the trail. It was much tougher ride than he expected, but reached the tree and boulder less for wear. After dismounting, immediately started searching for the backpack. It was not long before he noticed the large indentation at the base of the boulder. Getting down on his knees and peering into the indentation at rocks base spotted what appeared to be the backpack. By this time his heart was racing, felt as if it would pop out of his chest. Reaching inside indentation he grabbed one of the straps attached to the backpack and removed it. After retrieving the backpack, walked back over to his horse and hung it on the saddle horn on the saddle and then unzipped the backpack. Inside the bag, he could not believe his eyes, it contained bundles and bundles of hundred-dollar bills, wrapped in ten thousand-dollar packets. He immediately zipped the backpack back up and climbed back on his horse for the short ride to the farm. Arriving about the same time as the others, but richer by far.

Casually slipping the backpack over one shoulder, then dismounting and handing the reins to Miguel whom he thanked for his side trip, then proceeded to where the group gathered near the bus. No one gave him a second look. Once the driver took roll call making sure everyone was present, all were loaded on the bus and was soon heading back to town.

When they arrived at the tour bus kiosk near the beach, Sunshine got off the bus and headed in the direction of the bank. Walking into the bank when one of the banks executives happened to be standing near one of the tellers' windows approached Sunshine and asked, "May I help you?"

"Yes, I'd like to make a deposit in my account."

"I can help you. Come over to my desk."

Reaching his desk, told Sunshine to have a seat. My name is Reginald Kutsche "May I have your name or bank account number?"

Yes, "My account number is 9025200."

"Thank you, my name is Reginald Kutsche. It's my pleasure assisting you this afternoon. Before we get started, would you like something cold to drink?"

"Yes, as a matter of fact I would. A cold bottle of water would be fine."

The executive's assistant was asked to bring Sunshine a cold bottle of water.

In a matter of seconds, Mr. Kutsche had Sunshine's account up on his screen. "Will this deposit be deposited into the same account?"

"Yes."

"Fine. How much will you be depositing?"

"Somewhere in the neighborhood of one and a half million in US dollars."

"Fine, I'll get someone in here to verify the amount of the deposit. Afterwards, I'll be more than happy to add it to your personal account. This transaction shouldn't take long."

He walked out into the bank, conversed with a colleague, and returned to his desk.

Soon, someone be here shortly with the counting machine on a pushcart. In a matter of minutes, a clerk appeared with the pushcart stopping short of the desk where Mr. Reginald Kutsche sat. At which time Sunshine removed the backpack from the floor and handed it to Mr. Kutsche, who in turn handed it to the clerk. The clerk opened the backpack and began removing the wrappers from the ten-thousand-dollar packets; and inserting the whole bundle of hundred-dollar bills into a tray which when turned on counted each bill. Once the process had been completed, that bundle of bills was bundled in ten-thousand-dollar packets. As the last bundle was counted and bundled, the clerk manually counted the packets and wrote out the total shown on the money counter on a slip of paper and handed it to Mr. Kutsche, who looked at it and smiled.

"Everything seems to be in order. Give me a minute to enter the amount of deposit into the computer to your account. I'll be printing two receipts, one for you and one receipt for records."

After the transaction had been completed, Mr. Kutsche shook Sunshine's hand and told him, "On behalf of the bank, I thank you for your business. If there is anything else, we can do while you're here, please don't hesitate to let us know."

Sunshine left the bank feeling reassured things were looking up and he was going to be on his way home soon. He was surprised he was able in pulling off this bold escapade without Captain Eubank's interference. Sunshine hoped he had not been followed or Mr. Kutsche did not inform Captain Eubanks of his transaction.

Captain Eubanks would have been interested in how Sunshine could have done what he did—finding the money and depositing it in the bank without raising suspicion. But Sunshine thought about the Smiths, able to carry out several assignments through the Grand Caymans with little or no problem in the past. And all Sunshine did was find the money. *How lucky am I? My hunch paid off!*

But something still bothered Sunshine. How was it that Captain Eubank's elite undercover cops had suddenly dropped the ball? Sunshine had been shadowed by the Cayman undercover agents every time he left the hotel. *Why did they not follow me to the farm today? Had Captain Eubanks stopped tailing me? Did he want to give me enough rope to hang myself? Does he know what I just did? Is the cartel displeased with him for the way he had handled the Smiths? Does the cartel think he's the one that absconded with the money?*

It was a trying time for Sunshine. He was up to his neck in trouble with the Colombian cartel, the Grand Cayman police, and local DEA, and other local or international agencies which happened to be involved in such matters. He was beginning to wonder if what he had accomplished was worth the effort. He had been trying to turn his life around, but he had just gotten more entrenched in the underworld of misguided direction and intrigue. He wondered how he could live with the thought of constantly being scrutinized by the Columbia cartel, Grand Cayman informants, the FBI, DEA, and similar law enforcement agencies he was unaware of. *Will I ever be strong enough to weather the storm I find myself immersed?* He mumbled to himself.

He was still on the island, and visions of being found out, spending the rest of his life in a horrible Grand Cayman prison. *Could I be pulled from the line as I board my flight back to Chicago? Would Captain Eubanks really allow me to leave the island on my scheduled flight to Chicago? Has Captain Eubanks been in contact with the DEA? Is the DEA and Captain Eubanks in cahoots regarding my return flight to the states? Did the DEA or Captain Eubanks have a CI in the bank? So many questions, so few answers!* He knew he needed an amicable solution to this latest matter concerning the ill-gotten assets and this Captain Eubanks.

On Thursday, the day Sunshine was to depart. The alarm clock went off and instead of getting up right away, he laid in bed thinking of the mess he had gotten himself into in such a short time back on the island. Finally, he could lay there no longer and got up, dressed and stuffed what few belongings laying around the unit into his duffle bag.

He checked out of the hotel and took a cab out to the airport. After arriving at the airport and exiting the cab, someone approached him and asked," Mr. Lewis?" Sunshine turned and nodded, and handed him a one-way ticket to Chicago.

As he entering the terminal, he looked around to see if Captain Eubanks was there to bid him farewell. But to his surprise Captain

Eubanks or any of his henchmen were nowhere to be found. *So far so good. Safe for the moment. But it's still half an hour before my flight departs. Anything could happen between now and then. I'll feel safe only when the plane takes off.*

Soon over the PA system an announcement: "Flight 455 to Chicago will begin boarding at gate three in five minutes. Those passengers with tickets on Flight 455 to Chicago have your boarding passes ready." He quickly stepped in line with the other passengers along with his boarding pass, ticket, and claim check for his duffel bag. Once he was through the gate, and walking out the door onto the tarmac, was the first time he felt free in days. He was euphoric. He knew no other way to describe the feeling. *I hope I'm never subjected to this kind of mental anguish ever again.*

After everyone was aboard the plane and buckled up, the plane began its taxi maneuver down the runway lining up on the end of the runway for take-off. Once the engines were revved up and the plane began its short trip down the runway, air born and wheels retracted, he was home free.

Ready to return to Chicago and turn his life around specifically for his family's sake. He was ready to leave this latest chapter behind on the Island and look to the future and not live day-to-day. With only two options: turn himself in to the authorities and tell them about this latest escapade in the Caymans or did he want to continue on the road to uncertainty, which would eventually end in adversity.

Upon his return to Chicago, he had to weigh the pros and cons of his current situation, but at the moment, he was happy to be alive and back home. He had to do something fundamentally different with his life, but had to come to grips within himself before moving on.

If the Colombian cartel learned of my locating the money, they'll never stop pursuing me. By then, it will be too late for me. I could kiss all my hopes and dreams of a normal life with family goodbye. I have to make the right decision about which fork in the road to take if I want a future, a successful outcome rather than eventual disaster.

He wanted to talk it over with White Chocolate before deciding what was best going forward. Either way, it was going to be a life-changing decision for both.

CHAPTER 19

Arriving at O'Hare, Sunshine was met by White Chocolate and their two daughters. They indulged in a late lunch at one of the fast-food places along the way before returning home. It felt good to be back in Chicago.

As he looked at his family and saw how happy they were, he wondered to himself, *Will life ever return to normal for my family and me? If I make the right decision this time and do what's right, maybe I can finally leave that other life behind.*

At home, he sat alongside White Chocolate on the couch and told her what had happened on his latest visit to the Caymans. Astonished he had been able in locating the ill-gotten money belonging to the Columbian cartel. And was brazen enough to deposit it in their numbered account at the bank downtown. She worried his taking the cartel's money would cause more confusion and trouble in their lives, *was it really worth the risk?* She asked herself.

With this new worry, what would Sunshine's life be worth if and when the cartel learned he had absconded with their money?

After hours of pondering this latest fiasco Sunshine found himself in deep thought trying to decide the right road was to follow. A lot rode on his decision made now. After hours of discussing the matter, grudgingly he and White Chocolate agreed it was not worth the hassle keeping the money. After all was said and done, Sunshine and White Chocolate agreed to turn the money over to authorities. It was a difficult decision, but the only solution to their dilemma. In reality, there was no other conclusion—return the ill-gotten cash or run until the Colombian cartel found them and suffer the consequences. If they kept the money, the family would be on the lam forever.

If it meant remaining fearful of being found out, there was no alternatives; turn the money over to authorities and walk away. By doing the right thing, they would be able to raise their daughters in peace and harmony and live their lives without fear of reprisal from the Colombian cartel down the road.

Sunshine when he next met with Agent Goodfellow he planned to tell him about this Captain Eubank's and his close association with the Colombian cartel and the drug money he found and deposited in his account in a bank in the Caymans. It would not be easy to divulge his miscalculation to Agent Goodfellow, but he felt it had to be done.

The following morning, Sunshine visited Agent Goodfellow in his office.

"Welcome back, Mr. Lewis. How was your trip?"

"Fast and furious."

"Did you learn anything helpful or beneficial to the agency?"

"Yes. I think you'll be interested in what I have to tell you."

Sunshine gave Agent Goodfellow the whole story—the flight down, the stay in the hotel, the flight to Little Cayman, meeting with Captain Eubanks on his yacht, and going with Captain Eubanks to the cave. He mentioned the hunch he followed up on allowing him to locate the money then deposit it. And his suspicions concerning Captain Eubanks.

Okay, Agent Goodfellow said, "we need to keep you under wraps for a while as we investigate this Captain Eubanks."

Agent Goodfellow explained to Sunshine, "We need to learn everything we can about this Captain Eubanks, his role with the Colombian cartel and where he is in the pecking order in the Grand Cayman scheme of things. Sounds like he's deeply embedded within several illegal hierarchy down there. The government of the Grand Caymans will certainly be interested in learning about the captain's extracurricular involvement with the Columbian cartel. We'll work closely with the Grand Cayman authorities until this investigation is completed.

"I appreciate your assistance, Mr. Lewis. It will be up to the Cayman authorities along with our help and other agencies throughout the Caribbean to bring this drug and money-laundering business to a halt and hopefully this corrupt law enforcement officers to justice. Once the Grand Cayman government is informed of our intelligence, they'll need to take the ball and run with it.

"I'd hate to be in this Captain Eubank's shoes when they find out he's not only a corrupt law enforcement officer but also a CI, a go-between for the Colombian cartel. It's one thing to have having a dishonest policeman, but it's a whole other story to find one who's working both ends against the middle. That's certainly a new twist. He'll get his just rewards once the government finishes its investigation into his illegal activity. The government of the Grand Caymans will be all over his back as well as the Colombian cartel. His life as he knows it will be a thing of the past. I'm sure he'll spend many years behind bars once he's been investigated and exposed."

"What do I need to do now about the money?"

"First, we'll need to contact the DEA on Grand Cayman and let them know the state of affairs we've uncovered concerning Captain Eubanks and his group of thugs. Once this is done and the ball gets rolling, I'm sure they'll contact our agency letting us know what we need to do on our side as far as retrieving the drug money from the bank. They'll need time to complete their investigation and the impropriety going on in their local police department. After their investigation is completed and credible evidence against this Captain Eubanks is confirmed, he'll be arrest along with his cohorts. This type of investigation is long and arduous to say the least. Sometimes, it can take years to get all the facts needed to bring someone like this Captain Eubanks to justice. We first have to get all our ducks in a row and sufficient proof of the corruption among the high-ranking individuals.

"Charging the Colombian cartel will be much more difficult and challenging. They will need an informant in the cartel who's willing to provide information about the illegal drug trade involving Captain Eubanks. The informant will be at risk of losing his family and his life if his identity is exposed. Most individuals are not willing to do that for any price.

"It will all take time, but once the evidence is collected and the main participants are rounded up, the DEA with help from the local authorities arrest and charge them with drug trafficking and money laundering there and in the states if any of the arrested are US citizens. When the prosecutor's office thinks the case is ironclad, it will file the case with the courts. If the court agrees with the prosecutor's assessment of the case, it will schedule it for a hearing. After that, the prosecutor and defense attorneys along with their clients will assemble and choose a jury. Then the court will pick a date for the trial."

CHAPTER 20

After Sunshine's debriefing by Agent Goodfellow, he headed home where White Chocolate told him DeShawn called and wanted you to call him after you returned home.

Sunshine called the office, and Myriam put his call straight through to DeShawn.

DeShawn after finding out who was calling, first words out of his mouth were, "When the hell did you get back? And why didn't you call me the minute you arrived home? You said you'd be gone a few days, but it's been almost a week!"

"I got back yesterday, I was overwhelmed and exhausted. The trip took longer than expected. There were several unfinished issues that came up I hadn't anticipated. The business end of the ordeal bogged down and took longer than expected. I had to wait until certain matters were cleared up before I could leave. I'm sure you understand as a businessman how things don't always go according to plan."

"Yes, but next time, check in and let me know what's going on. Do I make myself clear?"

"I understand. I'm back and will be at work tomorrow morning."

"You better be here on time or you can kiss your job goodbye. I need reliable people to keep this organization running. If I can't count on you, don't bother showing up. Get my point?"

"Perfectly clear. See you in the morning."

The following morning, Sunshine arrived at the office earlier than usual and found Myriam hard at work. She told Sunshine, "Mr. Adams isn't in yet. But I was informed by Mr. Adams, as soon as he arrives, you're to meet with him in his office. I'll let you know once he arrives."

"Thanks."

Not long after that, Myriam notified him of DeShawn's arrival, left his office and headed down the hall to DeShawn's office.

Reaching his office heard DeShawn tell him, "Come in and take a seat. I'll be with you shortly."

After what seemed an eternity, DeShawn handed him a sticky note. Sunshine read what was on it and said, "I'll take care of it."

DeShawn finished his phone call and turned his attention to Sunshine.

"There will be a drop-off and pickup later this evening. It's vitally important to the organization that it be handled discreetly. Since you've been away, there's been a lot of unusual activity on the streets. Our CIs have spotted several federal agents nosing around some of our main drop-off sites. The word on the streets is that a large shipment of money or drugs is being delivered. The feds are aware of an exchange but not the location. We've been busy shifting our drop-off places the last few days, doing everything possible to confuse the feds and lead them on a wild goose chase every chance we get.

"Your job this evening is of the highest priority along with the secrecy of the drop-off location. You'll be meeting our man, Sledge Hammer, in a public place, the South Mall. He'll be waiting for you outside the entrance nearest the theater. This drop involves a large sum of cash, and I don't want any slipups. This exchange has been in the works for some time, and if it doesn't go well, I'll not be happy, and that means you'll not be happy. Get what I'm saying?"

"Yes, I completely understand. I'll be extra vigilant tonight. If I see anything at all suspicious, I'll walk away."

"It would mean a lot to me and the organization if you're successful in carrying out this drop. Your performance this evening is vital to the well-being of the organization. A lot of people are depending on you to make it happen."

"I understand."

"Now get to work. I don't want to see you again until tomorrow morning with the merchandise in tow."

Sunshine went back to his office to work on the paperwork that had accumulated while he was away. After spending most of the morning sorting through the maze on his desk. When lunch time came, he left the building, heading to the nearest pay phone to inform Agent Goodfellow about the big drop planned for the evening. After lunch at a nearby restaurant, he returned to work.

That evening, while Sunshine was standing outside the theater waiting for this Sledge Hammer, he spotted a suspicious character lurking near the entrance to the mall. The more Sunshine watched him, the more paranoid he appeared. *Who is this person? What does he have up his sleeve?*

Not long after spotting this character, Sunshine saw him remove a small caliber handgun from his coat pocket and walk into the mall. The store nearest the entrance was Radio Shack. Shortly after that, the man came running out of the mall, as Sunshine heard an alarm go off. He saw mall security officers on the scene in and outside the Radio Shack. Other security personnel were slowly driving around the parking lots. This did not bode well for the drop-off site, but if he remained complacent, Sunshine thought, maybe it was a godsend that this had happened; it would focus attention on the robbery and not on the drop-off.

Right on time, the courier Sledge Hammer appeared out of nowhere, coming from the opposite direction carrying a large attaché case. He approached Sunshine, who noted that the man was nervous, anxious to get the drop behind him and get the hell out of Dodge. Sunshine gave the courier the signal—a nod and a wink—which DeShawn had explained to Sunshine earlier.

The courier, spotting the signal, came straight over to Sunshine and sat on a bench placing the attaché case under it. A few seconds later, he slowly got up and walked away leaving the attaché case. Sunshine walked over to the bench and retrieved the attaché case; as quickly as possible, and made a B-line to his car. He opened the trunk, set the case down, closed the trunk, then crawled into his car and drove away. It had been a nerve-racking experience. He and whoever had robbed the Radio Shack had both gotten away clean and undetected.

The following morning, DeShawn, was waiting for Sunshine in the reception area as he entered, took the attaché case from Sunshine and thanked him for an excellent job. "Follow me to my office."

In the office, DeShawn opened the case and checked the contents. "Tell me how the drop went down."

Sunshine described the confusion at the mall the previous night before the drop and how relieved he was to have pulled it off in spite of the robbery.

"I heard about the ruckus where the exchange was to take place," DeShawn said. "It was a miracle that you and Sledge Hammer stayed as cool as you under the pressure and the drop was successful."

"I prefer working this kind of exchange in a more isolated or less congested location, not in malls or other populated places. Too much can go wrong when surrounded by so many people milling around, security cameras, local security, and so on."

"I agree. But having been identified or spotted so many times in the past, I thought we'd try something different. We learn from our mistakes. Next time, we'll be more careful where the drops take place."

"I thought I was going down when I spotted all those cops in and around the mall."

Sunshine returned to his office to handle more paperwork until lunchtime. When he left the building, he once again called Agent Goodfellow's office. He wanted to know if the DEA agents on scene at last night's drop learned anything helpful during the stakeout at the mall about how and why DeShawn's group picked locations or chose drop zones.

Agent Goodfellow said, "Every bit of information we gathered at last night's stakeout boiled down to this individual, Sledge Hammer, and how he operates and how and where he's contacted. It's one more nail in DeShawn Adams coffin as we slowly close the lid on his operation. Meet me at my office after work so I can go over the high-profile international drug and laundering case you helped uncover in the Caymans. I also want to go over the time and place of the drop scheduled for later this evening if there is one. I want to stay abreast of things as we proceed with our investigation. We still have a long road ahead, but we're making progress and the more we learn from the information you supply us and information we gather from other sources. The pieces of the puzzle are starting to fit together nicely thanks to you."

Arriving at Agent Goodfellow's office that evening, Sunshine and the agent discussed the mall incident. Agent Goodfellow told some interesting stats about Sledge Hammer. He had been a former drug dealer and just recently released from prison. The DEA learned his real name by running the tag number of his car. With this information, the DEA was able to add one more piece to the puzzle concerning DeShawn Adams and his organization. It gave the DEA more insight as to whom DeShawn's used as couriers. For the most part, he was using unsavory individuals such as Sledge Hammer only once.

That kept the DEA and other law officials confused and off guard; most of the time, they did not know whom they were looking for or whom to follow.

"But by having you work undercover for the department it has been a real eye-opener for the department," Agent Goodfellow told Sunshine. "You've been a real asset to the organization. Without your assistance, we'd still be in the infant stage of our investigation. But since you've come aboard, a can of worms has been opened, it's like we have an un-limited amount of intelligence to work of nights, and it's only getting bigger."

"Do you still want me to continue gathering information, or does the DEA have enough evidence to bust DeShawn and his organization?"

"Just continue doing what you're doing, Mr. Lewis. As soon as we feel it's time to arrest DeShawn and his group, we'll pull you imme-diately. We have a lot of circumstantial evidence but not enough solid evidence yet to convict DeShawn or his group at this time. Continue your undercover work. We should be ready to move on DeShawn soon."

"As you might know, we're working with several undercover agents in the Caymans. When that investigation is resolved, I hope we'll be able to show which organizations are involved there and extend here. So far, things are going according to plan, and things look good. Once we've made all the connections, we'll ask the Cayman court system to extradite Captain Eubanks and his cohorts to Chicago, where they'll stand trial along with DeShawn's group. It's a tall order, but that's what we're shooting for."

"If there's anything I can do to speed up the process, get in touch with me. I'll do what I can," Sunshine said.

"We couldn't have gotten this far without your help. After this is over, I'm sure you'll be generously compensated for your role. We may even find a way to hire you full time. Who knows?"

"I appreciate your candor, Agent Goodfellow. Never in a million years did I expect to be in this position. Even my partner is excited at what I've accomplished since leaving the drug business. Working for the DEA has completely changed my life. Thank you for this opportunity and above all for believing in me."

"All that has transpired in the last couple of years was made possible because of you and your commitment. If you hadn't come to us when you did, we would never have uncovered this international drug and money-laundering ring. We're still at a loss for words because it was under our noses all the time but we failed to see the handwriting on the wall. Between the Chicago and New York connections, the Colombian cartel, and the Cayman connection, this will be the biggest bust in DEA's history if we pull this off, and it'll be thanks to you."

Sunshine left Agents Goodfellow's office and drove home. When he entered his house, he saw Queenetta lying on the couch crying. "Why are you crying?" he asked.

"Mommy got hurt and is lying on the floor in the kitchen. I tried getting her up, but she just lays there."

Sunshine rushed into the kitchen and saw Cedrica in a fetal position lying next to White Chocolate. He noticed White Chocolate's breathing was labored. She was unresponsive. He took Cedrica to the living room and told her to stay with Queenetta. He returned to the kitchen and noticed White Chocolate's head was bleeding profusely. He realized he had to act quickly. He picked her up and carried her out to the car. He put her in the back seat and raced back into the house for the girls. He drove to the hospital which happened to be only a couple of miles away.

Entering the ER, told the first nurse he saw, "my partner is in my car parked out front bleeding from a large gash on the back of her head." Some staffers overheard the conversation and began pushing a gurney out of the ER to his car. Quickly as they could remove White Chocolate from the back seat put her on the gurney and rushed her back inside to the ER.

Sunshine had by this time removed the girls into the ER waiting area and told them to sit. He kissed them, and headed over to the counter to fill out the paperwork on White Chocolate. The admitting nurse told him after he finished the forms to have a seat with his two daughters.

Returned to where his daughters sat, told the two girls. "Mommy's going to be fine. Don't worry. She's in good hands now. The doctors and nurses will take good care of her and make everything okay."

He and the girls sat patiently in the ER waiting room for what seemed an eternity until a doctor entered the room and asked, "Is there a Mr. Lewis in the room?"

Sunshine said, "I'm Alfonso Lewis."

The doctor walked over and told him, "Your wife is not out of the woods. She's been heavily sedated and not in any pain at the moment. We've sewn up the large gash on the back of her head. We're running several tests on her to determine her overall condition. We'll be sending her down to have an X-ray of her head, upper and lower torso. It'll take a while before we have the results, but once we do, we'll inform you."

Sunshine thanked the doctor; he decided to take the girls to the cafeteria for a late dinner. After eating, the three of them returned to the waiting room waiting patiently for an update on White Chocolate.

A couple of hours later, a different doctor entered the ER waiting room. Since no one else was in the room, the doctor came directly over to Sunshine and said, "Mr. Lewis, your partner still has several issues we need to address before permitting her to leave the ICU. We've taken X-rays and done blood work to determine the full extent of her injuries."

Sunshine thanked the doctor for the update.

Later that evening, the same doctor returned to the room and told Sunshine, "We've determined that your wife has sustained a severe concussion and needs to be hospitalized for the next few days. She's had a serious blow to the head and needs to be observed around the clock until her condition improves.

"The X-rays also revealed liver damage caused by a hard blow of some kind. We've discovered through the X-rays that she's suffered a fractured tibia, the large bone below the kneecap. Since your wife has suffered multiple injuries, it's going to take time before she's well enough to return home. She needs to be kept sedated and comfortable, but once she's recovered enough and is able to get herself up, she'll need to go to rehab. I suggest you take your daughter's home and get some rest. There's nothing more anyone can do at the moment. We'll call if there's any change in her condition."

"I understand. It's up to her now to begin the healing process. Looks like it could be a long and difficult process."

"It won't happen overnight. We'll keep an eye on her, and by morning, we should know more about her condition. Until then, it's a waiting game. I hope she'll recover enough that we can take her out of ICU and to her own room sometime tomorrow. Until then, take care of your two precious girls."

Sunshine woke up the girls and told the them they were going home. He told them, "Mommy won't be leaving the hospital until later. She has too many boo-boos."

When Sunshine pulled into his driveway, he turned and saw that his daughters had fallen asleep in their car seats. He picked them up, took them inside, and put them in their beds.

Early the following morning, a nurse called Sunshine. "Your wife has been released from the ICU and is now resting comfortably in her own room, room 314."

"Can I call her?"

"No. She's still sedated and will be for the foreseeable future."

Sunshine thanked the nurse. He woke up the girls and got them dressed. They were back at the hospital within an hour. He took the girls up to the third floor and quickly found White Chocolate's room. The door was partially open. Sunshine gently pushed the door open and entered with the two girls. White Chocolate was lying in the bed attached to several machines monitoring her vitals. She was not awake, and Sunshine was not about to wake her. She looked so peaceful lying there except for all the lines attached to her body and a cast on her leg.

Later that morning, Sunshine called DeShawn and told him what had happened to his wife; he told him he would not be at work for the next couple of days. "Before I can return to work, I'll have to find someone to take care of the girls and tie up few loose ends. I'm sure you understand."

"Yes. Sorry to hear about your friend. Believe me, I fully understand your dilemma. Call me when you're ready to return. And good luck."

He then called Agent Goodfellow to inform him of White Chocolate's state. Agent Goodfellow told him, "If there's anything the agency or I can do, let us know."

"Yes. You can start with helping me find the SOBs who did this."

"We'll do our best to locate the person or group responsible. We'll explore all avenues we have at our disposal. That you can count on."

"I appreciate it. I'll get back to you occasionally and see if you have any information on who did this or why it happened."

He woke up the girls, cleaned them up as best he could, and made breakfast. It was not the same sitting at the table eating without White Chocolate. He was despondent and angry not knowing who had committed this cowardly assault against White Chocolate or why they had done it. He wanted to find out. He considered this as just another bump on life's rough and rocky road. He had had multiple bumps along the way himself, but he had always considered them learning experiences in the school of hard knocks. He always ended up with a better understanding of the mean and unforgiving world in which he lived. It was not easy living on the mean streets of Chicago, but he knew he had to experience the viciousness occasionally if he was to survive, and he and White Chocolate were survivors.

CHAPTER 21

In a few days, Sunshine was able to find a sitter, Imani, for the girls. Sunshine told her that she would have to be flexible, that his working hours fluctuated from day to day. Imani was willing to take the job and stay with the girls at a moment's notice. She was a neighbor who had recently lost her husband, and her two sons were grown up and moved away. She told Sunshine not to worry, that he could call her anytime and she would be available. The job was a perfect match for her and Sunshine until White Chocolate was able to return and resume her role as mother and partner.

Sunshine eventually returned to work. On his first day back, he was scheduled to receive a drop at ten that evening around Rush Street, one of the busiest nightlife areas in Chicago. It was full of wannabes, pimps, prostitutes, the rich and famous, and down to the homeless winos who had nothing else to do but wander the cold, damp, and dark mean streets. The drop was to take place in the alley behind the Charlevoix Apartments.

Before he left that evening, Imani told him, "Don't worry about the girls. I'll take good care of them. I don't mind staying a bit longer if necessary. This gives me purpose. Run along and do what you have to do. We'll be fine."

Sunshine called Agent Goodfellow with the information concerning the drop scheduled for this evening. Agent Goodfellow told him that DEA agents would be in and around the Charlevoix Apartments when the exchange went down.

"It's important that the drop goes as planned," he told Sunshine.

"That way, the DEA can gather more information about the courier and his association with DeShawn Adams group. Each bit of information the DEA gathers, the better the odds are of a successful arrest of local and international drug dealers which had been scheduled for less than two weeks. It's down to the wire. The DEA has to have all its ducks in a row to successfully execute such an elaborate takedown and apprehension of so many local and international players.

"Mr. Lewis, we're coordinating a bust with the Cayman and Colombian authorities. They'll be following our lead from Chicago. The different law and drug forces throughout the Caribbean area will be taking part in the roundup effort. It should be a good day if all goes according to design. We should be able to eliminate a large portion of the southern cartels and satellite groups not only in Chicago but also in Colombia and the Caribbean. The code name for the takedown is End of the Line. Pretty impressive, don't you think?"

"It is. Thanks for keeping me in the loop. If anything comes up or if I deem something important tonight during the drop, I'll inform you as soon as I can."

After washing up and changing clothes, Sunshine returned to the living room, where Imani told him, "Your suppers on the table. The two girls have already been fed."

Sunshine went to the kitchen and ate. He washed and dried what few dishes he used and put them away.

Back in the living room, he asked Imani, "Do you have anything important or pressing later this evening? If not, would you mind staying a little longer? I've been assigned an important errand to run later tonight and don't know just when I'll finish."

"I don't mind at all. I'm not busy. You go and take care of business. I'll have the girls wash up, and I'll put them to bed later. If it's okay, I'll make myself at home here on the couch until you return."

"You don't know how much I appreciate that. You've been a lifesaver to me and my family. Don't know how we'll ever be able to thank you enough."

"Don't worry about it. Do what you have to do. I'll take good care of the girls."

At eight that evening, he walked into the girls' bedroom and told them goodnight; he said he would see them in the morning.

He left the house and drove to Rush Street, where he found a parking space close to the Charlevoix Apartments. He was a bit early, so he just waited in his car until it was time to meet his counterpart. As he sat watching people aimlessly wandering the streets, he thought, *I see all types of people appear and disappear. The rich, the poor, the old, the young, the winos, the destitute, and the out of towners. They're all here.*

Most clubs and bars employed doormen who allowed some people in and kept others out. Most clubs had no cover charge but required a two-drink minimum of $17 per person and in some cases even more. Sunshine noted that most of those walking the streets that night was from out of town and had taken taxis from their hotels to Rush Street. It was a sham run between the taxi companies, the club owners, and the hotel doormen. When doormen were asked, "Where's a good place to go and have dinner and listen to live music?" They would say, "I know just the place." The doormen would hail a taxi and tell the drivers where to take the parties. Sunshine often wondered if the doormen and taxi drivers were playing both ends against the middle and collecting from the clubs. It was possible, anything can happen in Chi-Town.

When told by doormen to take parties to a nice place for dinner and dancing, the taxi drivers headed straight to Rush Street, the sleaziest part of town. There they would drop them off, and quickly depart. The tourists at that point would be too embarrassed or ashamed to turn around and leave once they had been left standing in front of a club guarded by a doorman. They would swallow their pride, pay the minimum, and chalk it up as a learning experience, a sign of the times.

As time approached for the drop, Sunshine exited his car and quickly ducked into the alley behind the apartments. He suddenly had an uneasy feeling that it was not a good idea. He was stuck in an alley with winos, muggers, prostitutes, and other undesirables everywhere he looked. He scanned the area for anything out of the ordinary before walking down the alley. When he passed a dumpster, he was jumped from behind by two men who appeared out of nowhere. They immobilized him quickly and put something on his face that immediately put him to sleep.

He awoke the following morning with a splitting headache in a small, dirty, and smelly room with two large muscular individuals standing next to him. As his head began to clear, he remembered that something had happened in the alley before he meets with the courier. He was sitting on a chair with duct tape covering his mouth. His feet and hands were tied to the rickety chair. He realized it was not a social affair, and worried he would not see his family again.

The aura the two strangers gave off caused him to think something bad was about to happen. He asked himself, *Why? Who's responsible for my ending up in this hellhole? These two guys are likely the ones who kidnapped me.*

He wanted desperately to ask the two individuals standing near him, but with his mouth covered with duct tape, that was not an option. He tried guessing who had set him up but came up with nothing rational. He could only think, *who are you, and what do you want with me?*

Neither man spoke; they just stared at him.

Suddenly someone knocked on the door, one of the men shouted, "Who's there?"

"Open the damn door," came the reply.

The man opened the door. DeShawn along with a couple more thugs were in the hallway.

DeShawn walked in and told the flunky who opened the door, "Close the f——ing door you idiot!" He turned to Sunshine. "I hope you've had a restful evening. Sorry you won't be going to work this morning. Since our last meeting, I've had several important matters surface, and my plans for you have changed."

DeShawn ripped the duct tape off Sunshine's mouth in one fluid motion. Luckily for Sunshine, he was still groggy from the ether or whatever the kidnappers had used on him, and the duct tape being ripped off did not cause him as much pain as it could have.

As his faculties returned and the pain subsided, Sunshine asked DeShawn, "What's the hell's going on? Why am I here?"

"It's like this, Mr. Lewis. Recently, I learned from one of my informants that you've been working undercover for the DEA. Is this true?"

"The DEA? No! I don't know what the hell you're talking about!"

"I think you do, Mr. Lewis. Why don't you start at the beginning and tell me what you've been up to since your return from the Caymans? I heard through the grapevine that you were involved with a couple in the Caymans working for the Colombian cartel and they stole a lot of money owed to the cartel. I also hear the money is still unaccounted for. I'm here to find out what you know about the missing money."

"I know nothing about that. While on vacation in the Caymans, my partner and I met a couple by the name of Smith, but I know little else about them."

"Oh, come on, Mr. Lewis. I know better than that. This isn't my first rodeo. I wasn't born yesterday. I've been in contact with a Captain Eubanks for the past month, and he's told me everything. Do I need to say more?"

"What did this Captain Eubanks tell you?"

"That when you went back to the Caymans, you met up with him. That he took you to some cave to look for the money the Smiths had stolen. He talked about a backpack you were looking for but didn't find in the cave."

"Really? What else did this Captain Eubanks tell you?"

"First, let me ask you why you went back to the farm the next day on your own. Did you know something you didn't tell Captain Eubanks?"

"No. I just wanted to visit the farm once more and take a photograph for my mate before returning to Chicago."

"What do you take us for, Mr. Lewis? Fools? We know you found the money and stashed it in your bank there. Captain Eubanks talked to your banker, a Mr. Reginald Kutsche, who told him he accepted a large deposit from you during your last visit. Need I say more? Why do you think I hired you? Not because of the assets you brought to my group but to keep an eye on you and help Captain Eubanks and the Colombian cartel recover their losses. The cartel wants what's rightfully theirs and asked me for my assistance. The cartel sent one of its own to your house to question your companion concerning the money. She was stubborn like you and wouldn't comment on anything about the money. If you don't want to end up like your wife and the Smiths, you need to tell me how the Colombian cartel can get the money back. That's the only way this nightmare you're involved in will end. The cartel as you are well aware is relentless. If I were you, I'd give serious thought about returning the ill-gotten money to its rightful owners and the sooner the better."

"Okay, I guess the Colombians have me over a barrel. I need to notify the bank in the Caymans so I can withdraw the money and turn over it over to Captain Eubanks to return to the Colombians. Guess I was outsmarted. I thought I could pull this caper off without reprisals, but I guessed wrong, didn't I?"

"Yes, you did. But you're making the right decision now. After we finish here, I'll call Captain Eubanks and tell him of your decision. I'm sure someone will be getting in contact with you soon concerning this matter. You're finished working for me. Get out of here and out of my sight."

Sunshine chuckled to himself. *Those are the sweetest words I've ever heard.*

"Go to your office and take whatever personal belongings you have there. I never want to see you again," DeShawn said. He told his henchmen, "Release him," and they did.

Sunshine walked out of the abandoned building and headed to the office to collect his meager belongings. After that, he drove downtown to meet up with Agent Goodfellow.

He entered the office and asked, "Is Agent Goodfellow in?"

"Yes, he is."

The receptionist paged Agent Goodfellow, who told her, "Send Mr. Lewis to my office."

Sunshine thanked the receptionist and walked down the hall to Agent Goodfellow's office. He knocked.

"Come in."

Sunshine entered the office, and Agent Goodfellow motioned for him to have a seat. He asked, "What happened to your face?"

Sunshine sat, still reeling from his latest debacle, and told Agent Goodfellow all that had happened to him in the last twenty-four hours.

"Mr. Lewis, we were set up in the alley behind the apartments. The agents saw you enter the alley, but soon after that, you disappeared. They scoured the area but came up empty-handed. The kidnappers must have taken you into one of the building nearby where they abducted you. I'm glad nothing more serious happened to you. All I can say is I'm glad it's almost over. We are close to reining in the bad guys, so you should be off the hook soon. All I can do at this time is suggest that until then, you go on with your daily routine. When you're contacted, let us know right away and we'll take it from there. I know it's been tough on you these last few months, but it's almost over. Be patient a little longer and we'll get through this thing together."

Sunshine went home and took the girls and Imani to the hospital to see White Chocolate. When they entered her room, she appeared to be sleeping.

A nurse came in and said, "Since your last visit, your mate's blood pressure has risen to an unsafe level and her breathing had become difficult and very shallow. The doctors all agreed she should be placed in an induced coma or become a candidate for a major stoke or possibly kidney failure plus blindness. This is the best recommendation we have for her in her present state."

The doctors on staff had all agreed that if she was to survive, something had to be done stat. They put White Chocolate in a medically induced coma due to her head trauma. They deemed it a necessary evil to place her in a state of deep unconsciousness to protect her brain from additional swelling. It was a gutsy move on the hospital staff's part but an essential one.

Sunshine, the girls, and Imani stayed in the room with White Chocolate for a few hours until the girls began complaining that they were hungry and ready to go home. Sunshine walked to White Chocolate's bed, took her hand, and kissed her forehead. He whispered,

"The girls and I are here, and we miss you very much. Hurry up and get well. We need you."

They left for home, where Imani prepared supper for them.

Sunshine told Imani, "After we finish supper, you need to go home and get some rest. The girls and I'll clean up the kitchen. You've done enough for one day. I appreciate all you've done lately. If I need you later, I'll call."

"Are you sure?"

"Yes, we'll be fine. Now go home."

She reluctantly put on her coat and told the girls goodbye.

After she left, Sunshine washed the dishes and put them away. He took the girls upstairs and had them wash up; then he tucked them in. He went to his room and cleaned up. He could not get the thought out of his head that he'd made such a mess of his life and that he had put his family in danger. He wanted to do something not only for himself but also for his family to rectify the bad choices he'd made. He lay in bed for what seemed to be half the night recalling the bad things he'd done. It was early morning before he was able to release those feelings of being a disappointment and finally fell asleep.

CHAPTER 22

Imani arrived early the next morning to sit with the children as she normally did. The giddy and giggly girls greeted her. She gave them hugs and kisses and said good morning to Sunshine as she passed him going to the kitchen to prepare breakfast.

Sunshine told her after breakfast, "I'll be leaving soon. I don't know when I'll be home. I have a lot to do and several places to go."

Imani said, "Don't worry about a thing. I'll take good care of the girls."

The first thing on his agenda was to visit White Chocolate. Then he would drop in on Agent Goodfellow.

After a short visit with White Chocolate, who was still in the induced coma, he left the hospital and returned to his car. He saw a yellow note under the driver's side wiper blade. Its block letters read, "Meet me at St. Anthony's Church near the main entrance to the parking lot no later than ten thirty." The note was unsigned.

Sunshine looked at his watch. It was after ten. He would have to hurry to get there on time. He headed for St. Anthony's and got there at ten twenty-five. He parked near the back of the lot and rushed to the entrance to meet this mystery person. He arrived at the entrance right at ten thirty.

He could not believe it when he saw Shanka, the waiter from Calico Jack's in the Caymans. Shanka stepped out from behind one of several large concrete columns supporting the church sign at the entrance to the parking lot and slowly walked to where Sunshine stood.

"Follow me to my car," Shanka told him. "Don't try anything funny or all bets are off."

When they got to Shanka's car, someone opened the back door. Shanka said, "Get in."

Sunshine bent down to get in and saw someone with a gun pointed at him. Sunshine reluctantly sat next to him. He had a feeling that he was part of Captain Eubank's band of thugs.

Shanka got into the driver's seat; they left the parking lot and headed downtown. They arrived a short time later at DeShawn's office complex. Sunshine was told to get out and do as he was told. All the while, the man with the gun had it pointed it at Sunshine from within his coat pocket. Sunshine did as he was instructed.

Entering the building, the three walked to the elevator. Shanka pushed the button, and the door opened. They got in, and Shanka pushed number three on the panel. The elevator began its ascent to the third floor. The doors opened, and Shanka pushed Sunshine out.

Shanka told Sunshine, "We're heading to room 321."

When they got to the designated door, Shanka pulled out a key and unlocked it. The man with the gun pushed Sunshine violently inside before he had a chance to do or say anything.

Once inside the room, Sunshine saw that it was some type of torture chamber. He saw handcuffs, ropes, menacing-looking shackles, and even large animal cages big enough for humans. Shanka pushed Sunshine down on one of the benches lining the walls and quickly attached shackles hanging from the ceiling to his wrists. He wasn't going anywhere. Shanka and his sidekick left the room closing the door behind them.

Sunshine was alone and scared about what was coming down the pike unless he turned over the cartel's money. The day had become one of the darkest and scariest days of his life. He realized he'd have to turn the money over to Captain Eubanks if he wanted to stay alive and keep his family safe.

Several hours later, the door to the horror chamber opened. DeShawn walked in accompanied by Captain Eubanks, Shanka, and the menacing-looking man with the gun.

Captain Eubanks glared at Sunshine and said, "We meet again, Mr. Lewis. Sorry it has to be under such grim conditions, but we must do what's right, right? I want you to give me your account number at that bank so we can return the cartel's money. If you don't, I'll have my men extract it from you one way or other in the most horrible ways you can imagine. If that doesn't convince you to give it up, I'll be forced to do unthinkable things to your family. I know you don't want that, so give it up now. Do I make myself clear, Mr. Lewis?"

"Yes, but I don't have the account password on me. You'll have to take me home to get it."

"Don't you have it memorized? It was your personal password! How could you not have memorized it? That's why the bank made sure you gave them a password that you and you alone would remember when you opened the account. The password should be embedded in your memory."

"Guess I wasn't listening close enough when they explained that part of the transaction."

"Okay, tell me where you've stashed your password at home. I'll have someone fetch it and bring it back. Then we'll call the bank and have the money transferred from your account to another account I've already set up waiting our transaction."

Sunshine reluctantly told Captain Eubanks where he had hidden the password.

Captain Eubanks pointed at the man with the gun. "Go to Mr. Lewis's home, retrieve it, and get it back here quickly."

Captain Eubanks had the man unshackle one of Sunshine's hands and handed him a phone.

"Call home. Tell your babysitter that someone will be arriving shortly to pick up some information you needed for work and to let him in. Then hang up. I don't want any idle conversation, understood?"

"Yes."

After Sunshine called Imani, Captain Eubanks grabbed the phone and turned it off. Sunshine's free hand was re-shackled. Sunshine watched silently as Captain Eubanks and his entourage left, closing the door behind them, and locking it. Sunshine reflected back on how he had wound up in this predicament.

The man Captain Eubanks sent to Sunshine's home arrived a short time later and knocked on the door. Imani answered it and saw a tall, dark, menacing stranger standing in front of her. His hat pulled down covered most of his head and face, and he was wearing dark sunglasses, dark clothes, and dirty shoes. He reminded her of a typical hoodlum.

He told Imani, "I'm here to pick up an important document for Mr. Lewis, he told me you'd be expecting me. I'm supposed to go upstairs to his bedroom and retrieve a document."

"Yes, Mr. Lewis called and said someone would be coming over. Come in. The stairs are down the hallway. His bedroom is the first door on the right at the top of the stairs."

The man squeezed passed Imani and headed down the hallway and up the stairs. In Sunshine's bedroom, he went straight to a large chest of drawers. He opened the bottom drawer and saw the small wooden box he had been sent to find. He put on latex gloves and removed the box. After opening the box, he located a small piece of paper that had been neatly folded lying on the bottom of the box. He unfolded the piece paper. The note was written in some kind of indecipherable writing or code. He put it in his pocket and returned the box to the drawer. He took off his latex gloves and stuffed them in his pocket. He went back downstairs and left without saying a word to Imani or the girls.

He drove back to Captain Eubanks and gave him the slip of paper. Captain Eubanks told DeShawn that it was time to revisit Mr. Lewis. The two and their entourage went back to room 321. Captain Eubanks asked one of his henchmen to unshackle only one of Sunshine's hands. Captain Eubanks then handed Sunshine the note. It was time to have the bank in the Caymans transfer the money from his account to an account Captain Eubanks had previously set up in Puerto Rico under a pseudonym.

He told Sunshine, "Do as I tell you. If you follow my instructions, your life as well as your family's will return to normal, but if you screw this up, it's over for all of you. Do you understand what I'm telling you? Have I made it clear what will happen if you don't follow my instructions?"

"Yes, perfectly clear," Sunshine said.

Captain Eubanks punched in the number to the bank; it was ringing by the time he gave the phone to Sunshine.

"Good afternoon. Cayman National Bank. How may I direct your call?"

"My name is Alfonso Lewis calling from Chicago. I want to speak with a Mr. Reginald Kutsche."

"Hold the line, Mr. Lewis. I'll make sure Mr. Kutsche is available."

Sunshine held the phone to his ear. It seemed to take forever before the operator came back on the line.

"Mr. Kutsche is busy at the moment with a client and will call you back as soon as he's finished. Is there anything else I can help you with?"

"Are you sure he can't come to the phone now?"

"Yes. You'll have to wait until Mr. Kutsche finishes with his other client. He'll call you the minute he finishes. What's a good number to call you back?"

"Hold on a minute, I don't call this number much, so I'll have to check to make sure I give you the correct one."

"Go right ahead. I'll put you on hold."

"Thank you."

When Sunshine heard the Musak come on in the background, he turned to Captain Eubanks. "Mr. Kutsche is busy at the moment with another client. When he's finished, he'll call back."

The operator needs your number along with the area code of your phone so Mr. Kutsche can return your call. We can do nothing at this time."

Captain Eubanks was hesitant to give out his private number, but had no choice; he was over a barrel if he wanted to get the money transferred by day's end. He gave Sunshine his private number.

Not long after that, the operator returned to the line, and Sunshine gave her the number. She thanked him for his patience and hung up.

He looked up at Captain Eubanks, who had a frown on his face as he anxiously waited to learn what had transpired.

Sunshine said, "Kutsche was busy assisting another client. I was told he'd return his call when he's finished with his client."

There was nothing they could do but wait for Mr. Kutsche to return the call. It became a waiting game. His call came about fifteen minutes later. Sunshine answered the phone on the second ring. "Mr. Lewis here."

"Yes, good afternoon, Mr. Lewis. I was informed that you had called earlier. Sorry I was not available when your call came in, but I was busy with another client. I apologize for the inconvenience and hope you understand. What can I help you with?"

"Thanks for returning my call. I need to transfer a portion of the money in my account to a bank in San Juan, Puerto Rico. I was wondering if it would be possible you could arrange to do that today."

"Yes, there's still time before the banks there are closed in Puerto Rico, plenty of time to help you with a transfer. If you would be so kind as to give me the account number and the amount of funds to be transferred, I'll make sure it goes out today."

Sunshine motioned to Captain Eubanks to hold up the paper with the coded number of the account on it. He gave Mr. Kutsche the account number of the account and the account number in San Juan, where the money was to be wired.

Mr. Kutsche told Sunshine, "The money will be in San Juan no later than four thirty this afternoon. Is there anything else I can help you with at this time, Mr. Lewis?"

"No, that's all for now. I appreciate your help in this matter."

Captain Eubanks took the phone from Sunshine turned it off immediately and was told to re-shackle his hand. He told Sunshine, "The bank in San Juan is to notify me immediately when they've received the transfer. When I get confirmation of the transfer, I'll send someone back to release you. If all goes well, you should be at the hospital no later than six this evening."

Agent Goodfellow had had Captain Eubank's phone tapped in the

Caymans and the US. The wiretap had secretly recorded many conversations over the weeks leading up to that moment—all conversations between Captain Eubanks, the Colombian cartel, DeShawn, Sunshine, and the latest one with Mr. Kutsche were all on tape. That was what Agent Goodfellow had been waiting for. It was the DEA's time to take the reins and begin the largest drug and money-laundering bust in its history. Along with international drug enforcement agencies, the Cayman DEA and other affiliates would be notified to begin a physical assault on each front once the transfer was received by the bank in San Juan.

It was just a matter of time before this ring was a fragment of its original self, but no matter how much these agencies tried to reduce the drug trafficking and money laundering, there was always a new group willing to take up the slack and run with it. The business was too lucrative, and the greed among its counterparts too strong.

Agent Goodfellow notified his DEA agents to be prepared at a moment's notice to begin Operation End of the Line. The bank in San Juan received the wire transfer from Sunshine's account and notified the local authorities, which in turn notified the DEA in San Juan, the Caymans, Colombia, and Chicago. That notification signaled the DEA and its international counterparts to begin rounding up those in the cartel and the splinter groups. Operation End of the Line was officially underway and would not end until all the main participants and players were in custody.

As the operation began its assault on dealers and the cartels, things did not go as smoothly as planned; there were many hiccups along the way, but overall, the bust was a major success. The majority of the main players were rounded up and charged with extortion, money laundering, drug smuggling, and countless other offenses. It was a great day for the DEA and other law enforcement agencies.

The DEA in Chicago arrested DeShawn and those in his organization and Eubanks and his contingent from the Caymans. The DEA and local Cartagena, Colombia, agencies arrested several notorious drug dealers but were unable to find the prominent drug baron responsible for manufacturing and distributing the illegal substances. He had simply disappeared. They would have to wait to arrest him another time. He could run but not hide; sooner or later, he would surface, arrested and brought to justice along with the rest of his group. It was just a matter of time.

The drug and money-laundering business had been suppressed. It was time for the courts to get busy and convict the dealers and those responsible for the illicit trafficking and selling drugs and laundering money. Several banks throughout the Caribbean region were included in the indictments and would be held accountable for their roles in laundering money for the cartels and dealers, but it would take months if not years to sort out all the details of the cartels and its dealers and get convictions.

At least drug trafficking in those areas hit hardest would be slowed to a snail's pace until new cartels took over the slack and started this whole scenario anew. Drug cartels would never stop producing as long as there was a demand for their product. That was a given.

CHAPTER 23

Several months later, after White Chocolate release from the hospital, she became desperately ill and returned to the hospital, where she passed away. That was a sad time in Sunshine's and his daughters' lives. It was almost more than he could handle. The volatile drug and money-laundering debacle was over, but he found it very difficult to make the funeral and burial arrangements for his beloved. It was another in a series of low points in his life. He knew that if he let his guard down, it would be over. He had to stay strong. He still had two little ones to care for. Without White Chocolate around, it was up to him to make all decisions.

He called on Imani to help him through these trying times. He had to reorganize his life and turn this latest dilemma around; he had to face his future with a positive attitude. He had to shift from a negative frame of mind to a positive one and continue down the new road he had chosen, one that would take him from the criminal elements on the streets, where he had once been such an integral part, to being a productive citizen.

After the funeral and burial, Sunshine returned home with the two girls and Imani. The first thing he did after arriving home was to call Agent Goodfellow and ask, "Is there anything I could do to help the agency? I'm available day or night."

Agent Goodfellow replied with a bit of doom and gloom, "Sit steady in the boat. If something comes along, I'll notified you immediately."

It was not long after that that Agent Goodfellow called him. "I need you to come down to the DEA office at your convenience. We've just received several new changes concerning employment in the agency. One new directive makes it look like you could be eligible for full-time employment here. Apparently, they've seen the benefits of hiring ex-cons and ex-felons in certain positions. You were most beneficial in getting this approved with your help in the huge Caribbean bust.

"If you're interested, drop by the office. Tell Louise at the desk that you'd like one of the new employment applications. Fill it out and return it back to her. After it's been processed and you are found eligible or qualify, I'll personally call you so you can come in and we can discuss your job. We can take the appropriate steps to hire you for a permanent position in the DEA. Does that sound like something you'd be interested in?"

"Yes, thanks! I'll be down there today if that's okay. I really appreciate what you're doing for me. I owe you and the agency more than I can ever repay."

"Fine. Come on down this afternoon. I'll tell Louise to have the application ready for you."

Sunshine called Imani. "I have to run downtown this afternoon and will be away for a while. Would it be possible for you to come over and take care of the girls until I return?"

"Yes, but give me an hour. I have a few of things to finish up before I can come over."

"That will be fine. See you when you get here."

Imani arrived as he was finishing up giving his girls lunch. Imani smiled at Sunshine and told the girls she was going to be there that afternoon. "What do you want to do while Daddy's away?"

Both started jumping and told Imani in unison, "Read us a story! Read us a story!"

"That's settled. A story it is."

Sunshine told the girls he would see them later that afternoon. He kissed them on their foreheads and told Imani, "Take good care of my girls. I'll see you later."

At the DEA office, he approached Louise, who told him, "Agent

Goodfellow instructed me to give you a job application. I suggest you use the meeting room down the hall to fill it out."

Sunshine took a manila folder from Louise and thanked her. He went to the meeting room and sat at the large conference table. He opened the folder and glanced at the many forms inside. He figured based on the number of forms that it would take him a few hours.

When he finished filling out the many forms, he returned the folder to Louise, who said, "Agent Goodfellow will get in contact with you with the results once he receives confirmation concerning your application."

"Thanks. I appreciate your help," Sunshine said.

Less than two weeks later, Agent Goodfellow called to say that he had been approved for a full-time position in the DEA. Sunshine was overjoyed at the prospect of finally having his first legit job.

Agent Goodfellow asked, "Can you could start work tomorrow?"

"Yes sir. What time?"

"We start work at eight thirty sharp."

The next day, he arrived on time, and Agent Goodfellow met him in the lobby. He took him down the hall and into his office to brief Sunshine on his new job.

"You'll be working with Agent Mahoney. He'll instruct you on your duties working the drug detail."

This was something Sunshine was all too familiar with, and Mahoney was a perfect match for him. He would be very helpful to Mahoney since he had been so involved with the drug business in and around Chicago all his adult life. This first day on the job was basic orientation; the work would begin in earnest the following day.

Spending the entire day with Mahoney, Sunshine got the gist of the job description down pat and was ready to begin the next day with zest.

The following morning, Sunshine met Mahoney in his office and was brought up to speed on the daily stakeout and what they were to accomplish.

Mahoney told Sunshine, "All we'll be doing today is observing activity in and around the Port of Chicago's waterfront. We have inside intelligence that a large shipment of drugs is arriving aboard a cargo ship docking at the port later today. Keep your eyes and ears open, and if you hear any chatter about a shipment of drugs or money, let me know immediately. We won't do anything until we're sure the shipment has arrived and know who's picking it up. We think a couple of crew members aboard the ship are transporting the contraband. Those we're not worried about. It's the ones they will deliver the shipment to whom we're after.

"When we get to the docks, we'll snoop around, ask a few questions, and get a feel for what's going down. If we're lucky, we'll be able to confiscate the shipment with the help of the port's customs authorities."

"Think I can handle that. I did a lot of covert work when I was involved in the drug business on the West Side. I think I'll be a lot of help to you and the agency. This is right down my alley."

"Okay. It's time we got started. If there's anything I can help you with, just ask. This is a team effort, not an individual grab for recognition. That's the only way we can get through this together."

"I understand. I'll have to remember I'm not Rambo, ha ha!"

At the port, they split up and started chatting with longshoremen as they ambled around the docks. They'd stop and strike up a conversation to get a feel if there was a drug shipment arriving at the port that afternoon. Mahoney had a sixth sense about who was or who wasn't interested in talking about such things as contraband entering or leaving the docks. He also had his own CIs along the docks whom he trusted for such information if called upon. The longshoremen were usually discreet as to whom they talked to and what they talked about. It was a dangerous place to work, and the longshoremen knew not to broadcast anything about smuggled goods in or out of the port because they'd face repercussions if they were found out.

Sunshine on the other hand was a little more brash about how he approached certain subject matters; he was more to the point. Looking and talking the part as conversations turned to drugs, he was a master and comfortable in his approach. He felt relaxed talking with the longshoremen, and they felt less apprehensive conversing with him about drug trafficking along the waterfront. Some he spoke with had kids who were addicted and wanted no part of the drug trade, which apparently ran rampant in and around the waterfront. With so many cargo ships coming and going, it was impossible to search every container large enough to carry packets of cocaine or money. For the most part, it was just sheer luck when someone discovered contraband.

It didn't take Sunshine long to develop a respect for the stevedores, longshoremen, dockers, dockworkers, and port workers. He had been unaware of the diversity of people and jobs there. The time he spent along the docks opened up a whole new world for him. He left that afternoon with a new respect for those who worked the docks and the tremendous amount of goods they handled.

He met up with Mahoney at the agreed time back at the car, and they recapped their days' activities. They had a couple of small leads but nothing substantial indicating when or where a shipment of drugs or money was arriving. It would be up to the customs officials oversee-ing the docks to inspect a small portion of the hundreds of containers arriving each day and locating illegal imports and smuggled goods, a daunting task for so few inspectors.

The following morning, Sunshine arrived at headquarters, and Mahoney told him that an inspector and his dog had located a large shipment of cocaine in one of Conex's that had been off-loaded late the previous afternoon. The container's manifest said it contained children's toys, but they opened the container and found the drugs stuffed into dolls.

The DEA and the customs inspector stored the boxes of dolls in a secure room alongside the dock. Other DEA agents traced the origin of the shipment back to one of the large Colombian drug cartels. At least this shipment had been confiscated; thousands of others were never dis-covered. Despite all the measures put in place by customs officials, the DEA, and the police, contraband continued to flow into the city.

Mahoney and Sunshine hit the docks again That day would not be just another information-gathering trip; they wanted to unearth what went on around the docks on a typical day. Mahoney told Sunshine to work the lower section of the waterfront. When Sunshine got there, he saw something peculiar and somewhat out of place, a cagey-looking dockworker sneaking between hundreds of Conex's. Sunshine saw him take bolt cutters from under his long coat and look around.

Sunshine watched the man cut off a lock and open one of the Conex's' doors and enter. The man soon came out with a small package under his arm. He closed the large door of the Conex and pulled the latching mechanism back through the eye of the other door and down securing the doors. He fled the area immediately.

Sunshine stayed out of sight as he followed the dockworker to a car parked near one of the main gates leading to the docks. Once he reached his car, he opened the trunk, put the package in, and returned to work.

As quickly as he could, Sunshine located Mahoney and informed him of his observation.

"What do we do next?" Sunshine asked.

"We need to inform customs of what you witnessed and together return to that car."

Mahoney and Sunshine gave the customs inspectors a rundown of what had occurred, and Sunshine gave them the make, model, and plates of the car. The customs inspectors got to work immediately, and it was not much later that the owner of the car was found and brought back to the car.

Soon, other customs inspectors along with Sunshine and Mahoney were on scene. One inspector asked the man, "Does this car belong to you?"

The dockworker with apprehension and anxiety in his voice said, "Yes. Why?"

"Would you mind opening the trunk?"

"Why?"

"Just open the trunk."

He opened the trunk. The unopened package was in plain sight.

Mahoney asked, "Could you tell us what's in the package and where it came from?"

"It's none of your business, man! Are we done here? Can I close the trunk now? I need to get back to work before I get fired!"

"You're not going anywhere," an inspector said, "until we find out what's in the package. Tell us where you got the package. If you don't, we'll open it ourselves."

The dockworker looked around quickly, found an opening between the customs inspectors and Mahoney, and bolted. He ran past Sunshine, who was surprised at the dockworker's boldness.

The customs officials and DEA agents instantly began yelling for him to stop, but he did not heed their warning. Mahoney and some of the customs inspectors who were armed drew their weapons and yelled at him again to stop or be shot. In a matter of seconds, shots rang out. The dockworker fell after being hit several times. It was not supposed to end that way, but Mahoney and the others had no choice but to take the dockworker down.

Mahoney called an ambulance. The EMTs came quickly, but the dockworker was dead. After securing the area, the police and crime scene personnel interviewed the agents and the customs inspectors. The car and package were dusted for fingerprints, and the dock area was canvassed for further information. The coroner was called to retrieve the body.

The customs inspectors and the DEA agents got permission to remove the package from the trunk and inspect its contents. The inspectors took the package to a secure section of the warehouse they worked out of. In the package, they found over three-quarters of a million dollars. They assumed the money was drug related, but they had no way of proving that. Illegal or not, the money would belong to the DEA once customs released it.

When Mahoney and Sunshine returned to the office that afternoon, Agent Goodfellow thanked them for a job well done.

Since he was involved in the shooting, Mahoney was put on paid leave until a hearing was held to determine if his shooting was justified since someone had been killed. That left Sunshine without a partner for the time being.

Agent Goodfellow told Sunshine, "You'll be working undercover for customs until Agent Mahoney returns to duty or we find a permanent position in the DEA for you."

The following morning, Sunshine drove out to the docks to meet his new boss, who said, "Welcome aboard, Mr. Lewis. I'm Customs Agent Long. I'll be your sponsor until you return to the DEA."

"Glad to meet you, Agent Long."

They shook hands and sat. Long read Sunshine's bio. "Looks like you've led a colorful life, Mr. Lewis. How did you wind up working for the DEA?"

"To make a long story short, I was instrumental in helping bring down a drug and money-laundering scheme between Colombia, the Caymans, Chicago, and New York. I'd been involved in the drug trade in Chicago and became tangled up with the wrong people and paid the price. I was fortunate to be chosen to work for the DEA because of my diverse lifestyle."

"I see. We can use your expertise same as the DEA as an informer. Since few people know you around here, it should be easy for you to go undercover and get friendly with the natives who work along the docks. They are a close-knit group, so you'll need to be careful not to blow your cover. Think you can help us out?"

"You're asking me to do the same thing I've been doing for the DEA, right?"

"Yes. We hear you're the best at what you do. You'll contact us daily by phone informing us of your findings. You won't be permitted backup or access to assistance. You'll be own your own basically. It's very probable that you'll expose yourself to danger and put your life in peril. Is this something you're willing to do?"

"Yes. I have two small ones at home, and I don't want them growing up having to face the same mean streets as I did. I visualize the rewards if I'm successful. They'll allow me to bring some semblance of order to my daughters' lives. Any task with uncertain outcomes is a risk I'm willing to take for them."

"Okay, Mr. Lewis. Now that you know what we need, we expect you to follow this undertaking with the knowledge of possible injury or loss of life. Just be careful. We'll be waiting to hear from you later this evening with a summary of your activities. Be careful. The docks are just as mean as the streets you came from."

Sunshine left the warehouse to see what he could pick up on the illegal activities along the docks. He was excited and yet terrified of the consequences this undercover work could potentially rain down on him. It was a dog-eat-dog business out there, and things could turn ugly at the drop of a hat. He had to be extra careful about whom he talked to and what he said. Since he had no backup, he would be an individual, in an all-out war fighting illegal contraband. It was a daunting task not for the faint of heart. He had accepted the challenge. As he walked alone on the docks looking for someone to talk to, he always kept in the back of his mind his two daughters growing up in a safer environment. It was worth the risk.

Over the next week, he fed the customs officials enough daily information to keep them busy running down each lead and detail. He gave them a better idea of the many new challenges they faced besides illegal contraband. Sunshine opened up a Pandora's box that had eluded customs investigators in the past. He had been able to gain the confidence of several higher-ups working the docks and get information others were not privy too.

It seemed that the drug cartels had people working not only on the docks but also in every key position concerning exporting and importing. They competed with the customs officials at every level, intercepting incoming and outgoing shipments of contraband before the customs officials arrived dockside. They controlled every aspect of the loading and unloading of shipments leaving or entering the Chicago port. They were aware of where and how to retrieve the contraband prior to most searches by customs. Items illegally shipped into or out of the port passed by them one way or the other as they were being unloaded or uploaded. They were always two steps ahead of the customs officials, but on occasion, customs were able to spread out in large numbers and beat the cartel to a shipment. It was a cat-and-mouse game every time a ship entered or left port.

Things the customs inspectors looked for during their searches included Cuban cigars, drugs, tobacco, alcohol, weapons, money, illegal immigrants, and items coming in or going out of the country without tax stamps and on rare occasion rationed items, the most underrated or highly controlled items on their list of priorities.

It did not take those working the docks long to start feeling the pressure of customs officials as they stepped up their unannounced inspections and to realize something had gone awry. Soon, there was pandemonium among those responsible for shipping and receiving contraband. They had to find the weak link in the chain and fix it before things really got out of hand and turned ugly. The only solution was to shake down the dockworkers, longshoremen, and anyone else with knowledge of or access to incoming and outgoing ship manifests or information from inside sources. It did not take long until those in charge had a handle on who the informants were.

Word spread rapidly among the dockworkers, and Sunshine's information dried up immediately. Dockworkers who talked about their work to anyone were removed quickly by the hierarchy. The spotlight focused solely on Sunshine, who was quickly identified as a CI working for customs. The hierarchy put the word out that Sunshine was no longer accepted or tolerated along the docks. Anyone caught conversing with him was dealt with severely.

Sunshine became an outcast as he roamed the docks and was no longer able to talk to anyone along the docks; he had become a pariah. After he conveyed his situation to customs, they sent him back to the DEA. His cover had been blown; he was no longer desirable as part of the customs inspectors' team. Even though he had been helpful in many respects, his expertise was no longer required.

CHAPTER 24

Over the next couple of weeks, Sunshine waited for a call from the DEA. With nothing else to do, he hung around the house caring for his daughters. They seemed happy to have him around for a change, and he doted on them.

But he was becoming antsy, and as time passed, he reverted back to the streets. His first job, if you could call it a job, was working in a stash house separating and packaging coke, meth, and assorted pills for sale on the mean streets. It was a remedial task for someone so well versed in the business as he was, but at least it put money in his pocket. He still had money in the bank in the Caymans, but he left that alone in case of hard times down the road.

In time, he worked his way back up to being a small-time drug pusher in familiar territory there on the West Side. His two daughters were well on their way to becoming college grads; they attended North Park University on the North Side of Chicago. Queenetta and Cedrica lived on campus and were rarely visited by their father.

Sunshine did not want them exposed to the explosive den of iniquity on the West Side, which had again become a hotbed of drugs and violence. Drive-by shootings occurred all too often. Violence broke out at the drop of a hat anywhere and at any time. Gunfire could be heard night and day without rhyme or reason. Too many young people were being killed or maimed. It was no place for Sunshine's two daughters. He sent them to live and study on the North Side to be safe. He wanted only the best for them.

Queenetta and Cedrica had taken different routes while attending North Park University. Both majored in health services—Queenetta in nursing and Cedrica in community health services.

Sunshine was proud of his daughters and their accomplishments at school. Upon their graduation, Sunshine presented each one with a bank account with a quarter-million dollars to use at their discretion. That was the only way he knew of rewarding them for their remarkable achievements.

After graduation, Queenetta moved to Sausalito, California, to begin her nursing career at Marin General Hospital in Kentfield, where she worked until she retired in 2014.

Cedrica found employment closer to home in Chicago, not far from the university, at the Community Health Medical Clinic. She dedicated her life to helping others. She is still working and is now head of the Women's Health Care Services.

Neither married, so there was no one to follow in their footsteps. Their father was murdered in 1998. The DEA and the police believe that the Colombian cartel was responsible for his death, but that was never confirmed.

Occasionally, someone in the DEA or the police department working cold cases runs across Sunshine's file and tries to solve the mystery surrounding his death but so far without success. He died as he had lived in a violent and troubling world on the mean streets of Chi-Town.